THE GUNS OF JUDGMENT DAY

Dan Briscoe had spent years building his name—a marshal who dressed like a dandy, gambled like a Mississippi riverman, and killed a little faster than any man alive. But Dan was thirty now—a long time to have lived one slow draw away from death. He was tired of the fear in his guts, haunted by the men he had sent to boot hill.

So Dan Briscoe laid aside his famous Colt .44s, took off his badge, and started travelling. It was in a bullet-riddled town called Springwater that his name caught up with him . . .

THE GUNS OF JUDGMENT DAY

Cliff Farrell

GUNSMOKE

This hardback edition 2004
by BBC Audiobooks Ltd
by arrangement with
Golden West Literary Agency

ISBN 0 7540 8260 1

British Library Cataloguing in Publication Data available.

Printed and bound in Great Britain by
Antony Rowe Ltd., Chippenham, Wiltshire

THE GUNS OF JUDGMENT DAY

CHAPTER ONE

Twilight of a blistering July day moved in from the plains while Dan Briscoe was making ready to take over his regular shift as night marshal of Yellow Lance. From darkness until dawn the responsibility of keeping law and order in this frontier town was his.

Yellow Lance was quiet at this supper hour. All sounds carried. As he splashed in the metal bathtub he could hear the voices of children at play. He listened to a housewife singing in her kitchen, the melody sweetened by distance. The fragrance of suppers being prepared on wood stoves drifted through the open windows. A dog was barking somewhere.

The thought bore heavy on his mind that this might be the last time he was ever to hear these homely evidences of tranquillity. This could be the night Diamond Dan Briscoe, Marshal of Yellow Lance, was to die.

Using scissors and razor, he touched up his small, dark sideburns and mustache, finding tiny imperfections the barber had overlooked. He paused to gaze at his hand. It quivered a trifle. Yes, he was afraid. He was thirty years old and did not want to die.

No doubt, the three men he was credited with slaying in gunfights in the past, had not wanted to die either. But they were gone from the face of the earth, and now it might be his turn. He was a gambling man and knew the odds were against him. You could not always win.

Therefore, he treasured this moment, which, to him, capsuled the good things of the life he wanted to live, but whose fulfillment had always escaped him.

He dressed with even more care than usual. He had an extensive wardrobe in keeping with what a man known as Diamond Dan Briscoe should possess. The city council paid him two hundred and fifty dollars a month to hold the lid on the town. In addition, he was known as the best poker player around. He could afford to dress well.

The day marshal was paid eighty dollars a month. Nothing much happened during the daytime in Yellow

7

Lance. It was a different story after the sun went down, especially at this season when the beef drives from northern range were coming in. Dan could hear the crash of couplings, and the fussy scolding of a yard engine as more cars were being shunted to the loading chutes at the stock pens.

He donned dark, tailor-made trousers, pressed to knife-edge crease, pulled on socks and bench-made, black boots with tops as soft as kid gloves. The boots had cost eighty dollars.

He pulled on a spotless white silk shirt with a pleated front. He snapped diamond cufflinks into place, knotted a black four-in-hand tie into which he placed a diamond stickpin. He pulled on a vest of watered silk and draped from its pockets a thin gold watch chain from which hung a diamond-set charm. He pinned on a gold marshal's badge.

Footsteps approached his door. A hand tapped the panel. There were two visitors.

"Good evening, gentlemen," he said as he admitted them. "This is a pleasure—I hope."

The two graying, elderly men wore clerical collars and the threadbare garb typical of the existence of men of God on the frontier.

Dan offered chairs. "How are you, Father?" he asked the Jesuit pastor. "And you, Reverend?"

"Well enough, physically," the Reverend Martin Pound answered. "The both of us. Mentally, it is another story."

"What seems to be the trouble?"

Father Dennis O'Brien sighed. "You know why we are here, Dan."

"Could be," Dan said.

"There's no need for you to go through with this," the Lutheran minister spoke. Both he and the Jesuit had been missionaries among the tribes in the early days of the trappers. They had been retired to this hand-to-mouth existence among their small flocks at Yellow Lance. They knew the frontier and its harshness. They had seen men tortured and slain. They had faced those fates themselves.

"What would you advise?" Dan asked.

Martin Pound hesitated. "You could get out of town until these men leave," he finally said.

Dan could feel the dryness of his lips, the brassy taste in

his mouth. "They're the kind who'd follow me," he said. "They're from Tennessee mountain stock. Blood feuds are tradition with those people."

"You could send someone else to arrest them," Father O'Brien said. But in his voice there was no conviction, only the realization that his mission was hopeless.

"You mean Frank Buckman?" Dan asked.

The two visitors did not answer.

"There's no other peace officer," Dan said. "Frank has the sand to do it. Too much for his own good, maybe. But he's too young. And too—"

He broke off, deciding not to finish the sentence.

"The word you were going to use was perhaps 'eager'?" Martin Pound asked.

"Eager to show he's as good a man as Diamond Dan Briscoe?" said Father O'Brien.

Dan said nothing. He could hear a late-arriving jerkline freight outfit creaking into town past his window. The acrid tang of wheel-churned dust lifted from Lincoln Street. Heat radiated from the town's frame walls. Lamps were beginning to glow in the business establishments. From Bozeman Street along the railroad tracks came the medley of voices and music. The dancehalls and gambling traps were tuning up for the night.

From his window he could see the wagon fires of Dakota-bound boomers blazing along the river. It was said that Sioux land was to be opened for homesteading. Some of it had already been claimed as range by cattlemen. Men would fight. Men would die. Other Yellow Lances would spring up. There'd be other marshals paid to keep order. Like Hickok. Like Wyatt Earp. Like Diamond Dan Briscoe, perhaps.

Cattle bawled and men shouted in tired voices at the shipping pens. More beef drives were being held on the plains south of town, awaiting their turn at the chutes. He could make out the shape of a chuckwagon where a cook was filling the plates of men in big hats by the glow of a fire.

Yellow Lance was shipping point for beef from three hundred miles around. Half a dozen crews would be in town after dark with pay in their pockets, after weeks of not having a roof over their heads, of not seeing a woman, of boredom, of days of pent-up energy and recklessness.

9

"What you mean, Father," Dan said, "is that I'm a bad example to young officers like Frank Buckman."

Martin Pound spoke. "Dan, is all this foofaraw necessary? All this—this flash and glitter? Diamonds and boots that few other men can afford? Silk and conceit? And, let's face it, a chip on your shoulder?"

"Arrogance, you mean?"

"If you want to put it that way, my son," Father O'Brien said.

"Even the Church finds value in flash and glitter," Dan said. "In vestments and in color and pageantry. And in arrogance from the pulpit."

"Don't be sacrilegious, Dan," the Lutheran minister protested. "Don't add to what you may have to answer for."

"Such as the lives of three men?" Dan asked. "When Judgment Day comes, I will have to stand on the record in the matter of those three souls, just as all other men will have to stand on their records. My conscience is clear in that respect. I've committed many sins, but I have never lied to anyone, except to spare them hurt. I've never cheated at cards. I've never taken advantage of unwilling women."

"I would advise you not to bring up the matter of taking advantage of women when counting your good points to St. Peter," Father O'Brien said.

"Unwilling women was the way I put it, Father."

More visitors were at the door. Dan admitted John Cass, Mayor of Yellow Lance, and the day marshal, Frank Buckman.

John Cass evidently knew the purpose that had brought the churchmen here. He eyed them, but they shook their heads resignedly.

Frank Buckman saw the message also. "Then you are goin' down there, Dan?" he exclaimed.

He gazed at Dan's garb with envy. He was tall, towheaded, with frank open features and blue eyes that held no secrets in storm or fair weather. He had stated that he was twenty-four years old when the town council had hired him three months previously as day marshal, but Dan was certain he was stretching his age by three or four years at least. Frank was driven by untried youth's desire to make the world notice him.

Frank added, "I'm goin' with you."

"This is my chore, Frank," Dan said. "It likely won't amount to anything. Making a brag is one thing. Backing it up is something else. They generally cave in. It's probably only whiskey talk."

"These are the Hatch brothers," Frank said. "They're not talking. And not drinking. They mean business. At least Jess Hatch does. He's the proud one. Dangerous."

"I'll take care of it," Dan said. "One way or another."

"I tell you I'm goin' with—!"

"And I tell you this is my possum to tree!" Dan said. "Don't you understand? I can't back down—"

He broke off. What was the use pointing out that Frank's own life wouldn't be worth much if Diamond Dan Briscoe didn't meet this head on? There'd be forty cowboys in town tonight, drinking and headstrong. The majority of them sprang from Texas stock, and their feud with town marshals was in their heritage, dating back to the days when their fathers came up the trail with the Longhorns.

There were other reasons, but Dan didn't mention them. There was his own pride, his own reputation, the image of invincibility he had built up. There was the fear that shook the nerves of opponents when they thought of facing Diamond Dan Briscoe. Arrogance, self-confidence, conceit. The diamonds, the suave, handsome, perfectly groomed law officer whose every movement reeked of superiority. That was the image. That was the impression Dan had nurtured in the minds of men until it had become his armor.

It had succeeded in the past. It had impressed faster men, caused them to avoid Yellow Lance, or to be law-abiding within Dan's jurisdiction. The image of Diamond Dan cast a long shadow.

"We could stop you," John Cass said.

Dan eyed him thoughtfully. "You mean by taking my badge away, John? It's too late for that, today, at least."

The Mayor turned appealingly to the two clerics. They shrugged hopelessly. "Pride is a terrible thing," Father O'-Brien said. "Do you want me to pray for you, Daniel?"

"If it would help you, Father."

The priest sighed again. He laid his hand on the arm of the Lutheran. "Let us go, Martin," he said. "We have only made his burden harder."

Dan saw the sadness in the faces of the two churchmen

11

as they left. So they knew that he was afraid. How had they discovered that? This time, above all, he had wanted the world to believe he was supremely confident, scornful of the men who challenged him. But they knew of the break in his armor.

John Cass and young Buckman lingered. "The clerk told me to tell you there's a lady to see you, Dan," the Mayor said.

"A lady? How could he tell? Do they wear a brand?"

"I couldn't say. He seemed to think she wasn't just another woman. She was a lady. She's waiting in the sitting room, I believe."

"That would be a real novelty," Dan said. "I've never met a lady. I'll see her later, maybe. If—" He checked it. He had been about to say, "If I'm still alive."

Instead, he added, "She'll have to wait her turn. What's *her* grudge?"

"She didn't say. But not everybody has a score to settle with you, Dan. It might be worth while to see her."

Dan walked to a guncase that was bolted to the wall. He fished a key from his pocket and opened the case. Hunting rifles and fowling pieces were racked there. Also a double-barreled buckshot gun, short and wicked.

A brace of silver-chased Colt .44s hung on pegs in cut-away holsters that were embossed with hand-tooled designs in the shape of sunbursts, with small diamonds at their centers. The pistols were flashy, expensive weapons that had been made to order. Their action and weight were balanced to the finest degree. The holsters, with all their outer display, were practically made of hard leather, with their inner surfaces smoothly waxed so as not to impede the draw.

Dan rarely carried more than one of these ornate weapons while on duty. This time he buckled on both guns.

Frank Buckman was watching every move. "Some day," Frank said fervently, "I'm goin' to show 'em a thing or two myself."

"Get out of this business, Frank," Dan said harshly. "While you're still young—and alive."

"You're still alive, ain't you?" Frank said, offended. "You've done pretty well at it. Fancy guns, fancy clothes. Fast horses to ride, an' women hangin' to your arm whenever you want 'em around. All the spendin' money you need."

"Everything's fast in this business," Dan said. "The grudges pile up in a hurry too, like the one festering out there."

"We can take care o' that!" Frank snorted.

"I tell you, you're not in this, Frank. This has got to be settled by me."

"Blast it, Dan, I could handle them two all by myself!"

"Of course you could," Dan said. "You could arrest them for carrying weapons off limits. They'd be fined a few dollars. Then they'd come back. I'm the one who's got to settle this, once and for all."

"I know how it'll be," Frank said petulantly. "They'll cave in when you walk in there."

"I surely hope so," Dan said.

"You an' your fancy clothes an' your three-hundred-dollar guns!" Frank snorted. He wheeled and stalked out of the room.

Dan looked at John Cass. "Frank's in the wrong business," he said. "He doesn't understand about the fancy clothes and the guns. He hasn't learned that you've got to make them *believe* they're in too steep."

"It takes a little more than that, Dan," the Mayor said.

Dan looked at his watch. "It's still Frank's shift by more than twenty minutes. I wouldn't want to try to make an arrest on his time. Pride is a fearful thing. For Frank. For everyone. For me. But it's worse when you're young, like Frank, and think you have to prove that you're tough."

He added, forcing lightness: "Suppertime. This is elk steak day at Ma Murphy's. Let's go."

He donned a hundred-dollar Panama hat, opened the door and ushered the Mayor out. John Cass was silent as they descended the stairs. The hotel sitting room was unusually crowded. The majority were men, but there were a few feminine faces in the assemblage. Dan was acquainted with the majority of the citizens in the group. He knew they had gathered to await his appearance. Some of the men were hunting and poker-playing friends, but none spoke to him. There was in all of them a sort of feverish curiosity. They were thinking that they were watching a man going out to kill or be killed.

After he had reached the street, Dan remembered being

13

told that a woman had been waiting in the sitting room to talk to him. No doubt she had been one of those who had stared with avid eyes. She probably had only wanted to boast that she had talked to the killer, Diamond Dan Briscoe. Likely, she would have asked for some memento of the occasion. A handkerchief, a button from his coat sleeve, a lock of his hair. Even a kiss. He had met with such requests in the past from women.

John Cass remained at his side. Their route carried them past Paddy Drake's Bar—a respectable drinking place on the off-limit side of town. Dan knew the two Hatch brothers were in Paddy's place. They were armed. It was against the code that Dan, himself, had set down for men to carry guns in this section of Yellow Lance. The deadline was Bozeman Street which faced the railroad tracks.

He looked again at his watch. It was still more than a quarter of an hour until seven o'clock. Darkness was approaching as he led the way across the street into Ma Murphy's eating place. He hung his hat on the tree and took a table at the front where he could look into Lincoln Street. Paddy's Bar was more than a block away, and on the opposite side of the meandering street, but still within his line of vision.

The eating house quickly filled up. Passersby drifted along the sidewalk, casting quick glances at Dan.

Ma Murphy bustled to their table. "I've saved some of the tenderest elk steaks you ever set teeth in, Danny, me lad," she gushed. "Young veal, cooled proper an' hung to cure in me own meathouse."

"More likely you had your cook slow-elk it from one of those beef herds down by the pens last night," Dan said. "Make sure, if it's beef you're wishing off on me, that you bury the hide and the brand it's got on it, Ma."

"As if, at my age, I needed advice from the likes of you," Ma snorted. " 'Tis coolin' down you need. I have just the thing for it. Beer that's had ice packed around the keg for two days."

She brought foaming steins. "Danny, you always was me favorite customer," she burst out. She wanted to say more, but failed. She hurried away, for tears had started streaming.

Dan lifted his stein. "Here's how!" he said. He had to force himself to drink. His throat was very tight.

He watched a man hurry into Paddy Drake's Bar. No doubt the word was being carried to the Hatches that Diamond Dan Briscoe was following his customary routine— a glass of beer and supper at Ma's place before taking charge of the town.

John Cass did not attempt to touch his beer. His lips were ashen. "There'd be no stones cast at you, Dan, if you ducked this one," he said. "At least by the ones who count in this town."

"You may be right, John."

John Cass gave him a startled look. "Are you saying that you might actually—might—"

"—Get out of town, John? If I did, nobody would get hurt, now would they? That's correct, isn't it?"

"That's right," John Cass said. There was sudden disappointment in his eyes. And a sort of accusing anger.

Dan laughed grimly. "Don't worry, Mayor. I didn't mean it. You'll have your fun."

"Fun? What are you trying to say, Dan?"

"You just cast the first stone, John. Deep down, you began asking yourself if Diamond Dan Briscoe wasn't yellow after all. The clay feet had been exposed

"Now Dan—!"

"You really don't want me to back out on this, John. None of you do. You'd all feel cheated. Disillusioned. Like children who'd seen somebody step on their rubber balloon."

"Then you *are* going through with it?" The excitement had returned to the Mayor's eyes.

"Yes," Dan said. He was suddenly very tired. And felt very, very old.

He sat gazing unseeingly into the street. Into Yellow Lance and its heart. Into its integrity and its faithlessness, its virtues and dishonesties, its blessings and its sins. In the three years he had been marshal he had become familiar with all of its facets.

He suddenly aroused, his mind snapping back to the moment. Frank Buckman was walking along the opposite sidewalk! He evidently had gone to his living quarters and had changed his garb. He wore a green silk shirt and a satin, flowerbed vest on which he had pinned his deputy marshal's shield.

A new, pearl-gray, wide-brimmed hat was tilted at a

challenging angle. He wore a pair of costly half-boots, stitched with gold thread into which he had stuffed the cuffs of tailored gray trousers. Dan had never seen any of these items on his deputy before.

Above all, he had never seen the pair of six-shooters Frank was carrying in new holsters slung from a heavy leather gunbelt. The guns were long-muzzled, with gold-mounted pearl grips. Specially made weapons that must have cost Frank more than two months' pay.

Dan surged to his feet, overturning his chair. "My God!" he exclaimed.

He ran from the restaurant. "Frank!" he shouted desperately. "No! Wait!"

Frank Buckman had already reached the swing doors of Paddy's Bar. He looked over his shoulder and waved Dan back. Dan's last memory of him was the glint of his defiant grin.

Dan was running. But the distance was more than a hundred yards. An endless space. He was still a dozen strides from the door of the saloon when the guns began.

His last steps to the entrance were measured by the heavy concussions of the six-shooters. "Frank!" he kept shouting hopelessly. "Frank!"

He shouldered the swing doors open and leaped into the room. He had drawn his silver-mounted guns.

Powdersmoke coiled in the room. The majority of the oil lamps had been blown out by the concussions. The few that remained were flaring and flickering.

Frank Buckman was huddled on his side with crimson staining the plank floor. One of Frank's fine new pistols was gripped in his right hand. The other lay a few feet away on the floor as though it had been yanked from his hand by the force of the bullets that had torn through his body. His hat had rolled against the footrail of the bar. His face was turned toward Dan. In the flickering light, Dan could see the frozen horror in Frank's handsome features. Frank Buckman had realized, too late, that he was too young to die.

A man was crumpled queerly against the far end of the bar, his knees drawn to his chin in agony. He was still alive and still clung to a pistol he had been using. He wore the denim jacket, jeans, and half-boots of a rider. He seemed as young as Frank Buckman. In his face also was the disbelief, the horror of knowing that he, too, was finished with life.

A third man stood at the far end of the bar. No other head showed. What few patrons there had been were still huddled beneath poker tables or back of the bar.

The third man held a pistol in his hand. It was pointed at Dan. Dan's guns were leveled on this opponent.

CHAPTER TWO

The third man was about Dan's age. There was grief and despair in his face. He was a man who had led his young brother to his grave. At that moment the brother rolled over on his side. His hands drummed the floor in the final throes of death. Then he lay still.

Dan did not speak. The one who had just died must have been Clay Hatch. The older man at the end of the bar would be Jess Hatch, owner and ramrod of a big cattle outfit, whose brand was the Bar K, and whose headquarters were on Wind River, far away.

The thought came to Dan that he would not have known either of these men who had come here to kill him if he had met them on the street. Nor, no doubt, would they have recognized him as the officer they had sworn they would kill. This was the first time they had met, face-to-face.

Evidently they had taken it for granted that the badge-wearing man, garbed so flashily, who had stepped into the saloon, had been Diamond Dan Briscoe.

"You've killed the wrong man, Hatch," Dan said. "He was my deputy. Just a young man who wanted to grow up too fast. I'm Dan Briscoe. I'm the one you were looking for."

Jess Hatch did not move for seconds. In him was a sickness and a guilt. He had come here to avenge the death of one of his riders who had been killed by a bullet from Dan's six-shooter in this same saloon a year in the past. A year to the day, almost to the minute. Palpably, this was the way Jess Hatch had timed it. It was to have been his tribute to one of his Bar K cowboys who had tried to defy the law and Diamond Dan Briscoe.

"I tuk my solemn word on the Book I'd kill you, Briscoe," Jess Hatch finally said. "I look after my riders."

"An oath on the Book is a hard thing for a man like you to renounce," Dan said.

"Young Stevie Webb was more'n a man who worked for me," Jess Hatch said. "He was a friend."

"Pull that trigger, and we'll both go," Dan said. "Would that make Stevie Webb sleep easier in his grave?"

"He was drunk that day," Jess Hatch said. "You could have spared him. He had no chance ag'in the likes o' you."

"He was drunk," Dan said. "But not too drunk. That kind are the hardest to deal with. He shot twice at me before I pulled a trigger. You won't believe this, but I shot two feet wide of him, trying only to scare him. But he dove for cover. My slug glanced from that cannon stove there to your right. It went through his heart. You can see the scar on the stove to this day."

Jess Hatch remained silent for seconds. Then he lowered his gun. He was a homely, box-jawed man, leaned and leathered by weather and hardship. He moved to where his brother's body lay and knelt beside it. He began to sob.

"My God, Clay!" he choked. "Oh, my God!"

Dan bent over Frank Buckman. Frank was dead. Two bullets had smashed through his chest. Dan straightened, leaving Frank there with that horrible disbelief frozen in his face.

Other men came sidling cautiously into the room. Someone brought a blanket and started to cover Clay Hatch's body. Jess Hatch pushed it aside. He lifted his brother in his arms. Still sobbing, he walked out of the place with his burden. He said, in agony, "Oh, damn it all! Why wasn't it me? Why wasn't it me that had to go?"

Dan felt John Cass's hand on his arm. He let himself be led out of the saloon and to the Mayor's office. John Cass locked the door, and drew a bottle of whiskey and glasses from a cabinet. "You could use this, Dan," he said, pouring a drink.

Dan waved it away. From a window, he watched Jess Hatch carry his brother down Lincoln Street, and turn the corner into the hurrah district on Bozeman Street. Torchlight still glowed there, but the gunfire uptown had muted the music and the sounds of revelry.

"I could still arrest him," he said. "He broke the law. But he's been punished enough." He added, "More than enough."

A new procession came from Paddy's Bar. Frank Buckman's body, covered by a sheet, was carried on a stretcher, followed by a straggle of townspeople. There were women among the group. None was weeping. They were only excited and avidly curious.

The stretcher was borne into Henry Adams' undertaking parlor. The group still swirled around the door, chattering.

"Frank shouldn't have tried to back down the Hatch brothers," John Cass said. "And why did he want to get rigged out in all that fancy? He—"

Dan interrupted him. "Frank had folks back in Nebraska. His parents and a sister, I believe. Farm people. They must be notified."

"I'll take care of it," John Cass said.

"Bury him in his fancy clothes, and wearing his two guns."

"That might not be fitting," the Mayor protested.

"That's the way Frank would want it," Dan said.

He unstrapped his two guns, removed his marshal's shield and placed them on the Mayor's desk. "These things were only a front anyway," he said. "It wasn't me they feared. It was the reputation, not the man. They never looked beyond the tinsel."

"Hold on, Dan! You're not quitting?"

"That's the exact word for it, John. Quitting. I had made up my mind to step out weeks ago. Then I heard the Hatch brothers had taken oath to pay me off. So I stayed. I had strutted too long. I was really beginning to believe in Diamond Dan Briscoe. To believe I was invincible. If I'd quit then, those two young men would be alive now."

"You're not looking at this right, Dan. If Frank had stayed out of it, likely there never would have been any shooting. He forced the fight. I doubt if the Hatches would have gone through with it against a man of your record, if Frank hadn't crowded them."

"A man of my record, John? Just what is my record?"

The Mayor frowned, started to speak, then went silent.

"They say I've killed five or six men," Dan said. "Or is it

19

a dozen now? Each time I hear it the number grows bigger. The truth is I never killed a human being in my life."

The Mayor decided he was not being serious, and started to laugh uneasily. The laugh died. "What do you mean, Dan? What about—?"

"The three men they say I rubbed out here in Yellow Lance? One was a whiskey-crazed bullwhacker who went berserk on the street the first month I was marshal. He had killed two innocent people, and was about to kill a woman. I shot him. Then there was a rat-faced footpad I found rifling the pockets of a man he had slugged back of a saloon. He's on the list of those I'm supposed to have killed."

"Supposed?"

"That thief was killed by his own gun, John. I traded shots with him in the darkness as he ran. He fell over an ash heap and dropped his gun. It exploded and the bullet hit him between the eyes. The way it's told, that was a perfect example of how handy Diamond Dan Briscoe is with a gun. The truth is, I was shooting in another direction. I didn't even know where he was in the darkness."

He watched the Mayor's blank expression. "Up to now, I'm the only person who knew that," he continued. "As for the bullwhacker, I shot him in the leg. It knocked him down, but it was only a flesh wound. It saved the life of the woman he was threatening, but he died in Doc Petticord's office. It wasn't my slug that killed him. Alcohol poisoning was the real cause. Doc Petticord will tell you that. It's been sort of a secret between us. You might call it a joke. As for that cowboy, Steve Webb, my bullet killed him, but it was an accident. A ricochet."

He walked to a window and gazed down into Yellow Lance's street. "That's the record," he said slowly. "Diamond Dan Briscoe's record as a killer. An alcoholic who died of the DTs, a stumblebum who fell on his own gun, a young cowpuncher who was unlucky."

"But, how about the—the others?" John Cass asked hollowly.

"What others?"

"Everybody says that you . . ." The Mayor's voice again faded.

"You mean the ones they say I killed before I became marshal here? There weren't any, John. That was just barroom talk. As a deputy in Cheyenne and a few other places

I had built myself a rep as a gunslinger and a tough law man. It was an image I created. I just let my rep grow as all weeds grow. It was worth money to me. Two hundred and fifty dollars a month here in Yellow Lance. But, it was worth more than money. It protected my life. It made my job easier. Not until the Hatches showed up today, did anyone really have the sand to try to call my bluff."

There was a long silence. John Cass poured himself a drink and downed it. "No, Dan," he finally said. "It wasn't a bluff, and they knew it. That's the real reason why they steered clear of you until today."

Dan shrugged. "Father O'Brien and Martin Pound were right. I set a bad example for an ambitious young deputy who wanted to prove he was as good a man as Diamond Dan Briscoe. Me and my strut and my swagger. I'll tell you something, John, that I wish Frank had known."

"You don't have to tell me anything, Dan."

"Every night when I took over the shift, I was scared. Every time I walked up to an armed man to make an arrest, I was afraid."

He added, "Maybe, if Frank had known that, he might have learned to be scared too. He might still be alive. And so might Clay Hatch. Then I'd only have to explain about the other three when Judgment Day comes. Now I've got two more lives written against me."

He unlocked the door and left the office. Groups still lingered along the sidewalks. The aftermath of the shooting was like dying smoke in the town. A new stir of interest ran along the street when Dan appeared. A few men tried to speak to him, but he brushed past and walked to the hotel where he roomed.

As he passed through the lobby, he recalled something. He paused at the desk. "I was told there had been a lady who wanted to see me," he said to the clerk.

"Lady?" the man said thoughtfully. "Not to my knowledge, Dan."

John Cass evidently had been mistaken. Or, perhaps, another clerk had been on duty earlier. It didn't matter. The sitting room was vacant now. Nothing mattered.

Dan attended graveside services for Frank Buckman late the next afternoon. A large gathering of town people bowed their heads as the Reverend Martin Pound read the

Lutheran service. A choir sang a hymn. The consecration was performed, and the exodus began from the cemetery where a few acres had been cleared in the bleak vastness of buffalo grass and sagebrush, and fenced with barbed wire to keep out the range stock.

Dan was among the last to turn away. Clay Hatch had been buried earlier in the day in the opposite corner of the graveyard. The fresh mound bore a wreath which was already withering in the hot, plains wind.

Dan walked to this grave. It had been dug alongside a year-old mound, now sunken. At its head stood a wooden head board on which, in painted letters, was the information that here lay Steven Joseph Webb, born in Grundy County, Tennessee, who had gone to sit at the feet of his Maker at the age of twenty-two.

Dan stood, remembering the night his glancing bullet had taken the life of this young cowboy. Like all the others, Steve Webb had been a complete stranger to him at the moment of decision. He had been a wild, undisciplined youth who had scorned the law and resisted restraint in his desire to be noticed by other men. Now his friend, Clay Hatch, had joined him in this lonely, alien place.

Dan discovered he was not alone. Jess Hatch stood a dozen feet away. They gazed at each other in silence.

"I'm sorry," Dan finally said. "More than I can put into words. More than you'd believe, I'm afraid."

Jess Hatch drew a long breath. "Yes, I could believe," he said. "I've learned, too late, what real sorrow is. I brought him to his death. Me an' my damned pride."

He was not armed. Dan turned and walked away toward the lights of Yellow Lance that were beginning to bloom in the dusk. That grudge, at least, was finished. But there likely were others that would follow him.

He found John Cass waiting for him, and they walked together into town. "What are you going to do, Dan?" the Mayor asked.

"Go somewhere," Dan said. "And change my name."

"Change your name? Is that necessary?"

"Is there any other way to clean the slate?"

"You've got no slate to clean."

"I've stepped on a lot of toes. Some men never forget. That's one of the penalties for taking a law job. I want to rub off the target that's painted on my back. It's there. I can feel it."

"Have you got any special place in mind, Dan?"

"No. Just a place so far away they never heard of Yellow Lance or Diamond Dan Briscoe."

"That's what I want to talk about to you," John Cass said. "This is somewhat of a coincidence. Have you ever heard of Springwater Basin?"

"Can't say I have."

"I figured you hadn't. Have you ever punched cows, Dan?"

"Some. I was raised on a patch-saddle outfit in the Nebraska sandhills by an uncle who took me in after my parents died when I was chin-high to a stirrup. I know which end of a throw rope to dab around a steer. I've doctored screwworm and glanders."

"What I've got in mind is a fair-sized ranch that's in need of a good man who can eventually take over and run the outfit. You could let the hands do the roping and doctoring."

"I hardly had cattle ranching in mind, John. But, where is this Springwater Basin?"

"Arizona. There's a town named Flat Butte in the middle of the basin. Does that mean anything to you?"

"No," Dan said. "Arizona? That *is* a long, far, shout from here. I'm not much for living on a desert, John. I'm a prairie dog."

"I see that you've never been to Arizona. But I have. And to Springwater Basin. Arizona isn't all desert by a long shot. And the basin is as pretty a cow country as you'll ever lay eyes on. I was there years ago for a short time. I'd be willing to bet a tin dime there's only one person down there who ever heard of Yellow Lance, let alone Diamond Dan Briscoe. And the only reason is that he happens to be an old friend of mine. We keep in touch with each other."

"I'm listening," Dan said.

"His name is Bill Royal and he owns an outfit called the Spanish Bell in the basin. Bill and I were prospecting partners in Arizona in the 'Pache days, but he quit prospecting when he saw the basin, and went to ranching. It happened that I got a letter from him a couple of weeks ago, asking me to keep a looksee for a reliable man who might like a job that would pay top wages and who had the savvy to work into a foreman's job. There might even be a partnership in it for the right man in the future. Bill's all stove up and can't ride. He's up in his sixties, and the outfit's too much for his daughter to handle."

"Daughter?"

"Katey Royal. She's a widow woman. Riding help is hard to find in that country. It's miles from nowhere. Bill's letter had slipped my mind until you mentioned you was quitting. I sort of figured a place like the basin might suit you."

"I'd have to think it over," Dan said. "Just how would a man get to this place?"

"I've got a map in my office," the Mayor said. "We'll take a look at it."

Dan studied the map the Mayor spread on a desk. "The nearest railroad point is a town called Flag on the Santa Fe main line," the Mayor explained. "From Flag you take stage south to Flat Butte in the basin."

Dan rubbed his chin. "I was aiming on heading for California anyway," he said. "This wouldn't be far off my trail. I just might stop off and take a look at Springwater Basin. It's got a right pretty ring. What did you say was the name of this ranch?"

"Spanish Bell. I'll send a telegram to Katey and her father, telling them—"

Dan halted him. "Don't send word of any kind. I'll probably change my mind and never show up there anyway. Even if I do I don't want anyone to know I was Dan Briscoe from Yellow Lance. If I get to Flat Butte, I want to be only a common cowhand looking for a riding job. I'll hold you to this, John."

They shook hands on it, and Dan turned to leave the office. "Wait!" the Mayor exclaimed. "How about your guns? I've still got them. You left them here yesterday."

"Give them to the new night marshal, whoever he is," Dan said. "They might help keep him alive."

CHAPTER THREE

It was two weeks later when Dan Briscoe alighted from a west-bound Santa Fe express at a station which had the name, FLAG, painted on its wall.

At first, after his talk with John Cass, he had shrugged off any notion of acting on his suggestion. But that name, Springwater Basin, had kept running through his mind. It sounded peaceful. It sounded right. Finally, still doubting that he would ever really go through with visiting the place, he had bought his ticket from Kansas City only as far as Flag.

He gazed around. A late afternoon sun hung in a sky so blue it seemed unreal. White clouds with flat undersides floated above table-topped mesas. A thick pine forest clothed the flats and climbed the slopes at the bases of the mesas. Blanket Indians squatted against the depot wall. Giggling Hopi squaws made remarks to each other in their own tongue about these train-weary strangers who stampeded from the coaches into the Fred Harvey restaurant in the depot. There, waitresses in starched aprons and white caps became busy.

Dan got his bedroll and leather satchel from the baggage truck, then moved into the shade of the depot while he surveyed the town. Like the other passengers, he was wrinkled and dusty after days aboard a train rolling through the oven heat of Kansas and New Mexico. He needed a shave, but his mustache and sideburns were gone. Along with many other things in his past he had shed them before boarding the train.

Protected from the sun, he found the air surprisingly cool and bracing. Also thin. This was mountain country. A sign on the depot stated that Flag's elevation was 7255 feet above sea level. Population 358.

A sawmill droned somewhere, sending forth the spice of resin to tone up the fragrance of the pines. A distant, snow-tipped mountain peak was framed by the sky. There was only one jarring note. In addition to lumbering, Flag was a railroad town, and a shipping point for cattle. There were pens and loading chutes in sight down the tracks. That reminded him of Yellow Lance.

He was almost of a mind to return to the train and continue the journey westward. But he found himself responding to the country.

He searched out the sign of a Wells Fargo office near the depot and walked there, carrying his belongings. He wore a white cotton shirt and the customary denim saddle breeches and half-boots. Like his bedroll and the satchel, both of which he had bought secondhand in Kansas City, his attire showed the fading and wear of much use and many washings. It had seen many hunting trips when he had been off duty at Yellow Lance, as had the seasoned range hat that shaded his face.

Several cow ponies were tethered at rails of stores and saloons along the dusty street. Cowhands were commonplace in Flag. He drew scarcely a second glance from passersby.

The stage office seemed deserted, but the sound of his heels on the plank floor, brought a bald head rising reluctantly beyond the counter. The agent, who had been dozing in a chair, got to his feet with an abused sigh. He had a wrinkled, petulant face, and the apathy of a man not in love with his job. "What is it?" he barked.

"I'm thinkin' of headin' for Flat Butte, if there's a stage in that direction," Dan said.

The pouting lips straightened. Tired eyes suddenly became inquisitive. "Flat Butte, hey?"

Dan waited. When the man didn't elaborate on the query, he nodded. "That's it. Flat Butte."

The agent placed elbows on the counter in order to pull his body higher so that he could lean and inspect Dan from head to foot. "Cowhand?" he asked.

"I reckon," Dan said. "Now, about a stage to Flat Butte?"

"You'll have to wait a couple days," the agent said. "Stage to Flat Butte an' points south leaves here only on Tuesdays an' Fridays. This is Wednesday. Next one pulls out Friday mornin' at five-thirty sharp."

"What's the fare?" Dan asked.

"One way?"

There was malicious irony in the question. Dan found himself wanting to twist the sharp, little nose that was poked in his direction. "I haven't decided," he said.

26

"Twelve-fifty, one way," the agent said. "Twenty-four dollars round trip. You'll save a dollar."

"I'll let you know," Dan said.

"I'd advise a round trip," the man said.

"Now, if there's one thing that doesn't cost a man a cent, it's giving advice, good or bad," Dan remarked.

"An' worth a lot more'n money, sometimes, mister," the agent snapped.

Dan left the office, pondering the man's attitude. There was, of course, the chance he had been recognized, but he doubted if that was the real explanation. He headed toward a ramshackle, two-story structure on the opposite side of the street whose sign proclaimed it as offering rooms and board. It was named Heather House.

A sizable wagon, with a canvas top sagging over narrow hoops, was entering town from the west, drawn by a six-horse team. Its body rumbled and boomed as it negotiated the chuckholes, showing that the vehicle was traveling empty.

It was accompanied by two outriders on chunky horses that were wild-eyed and trying to refuse entering the lane of buildings. The riders, as well as the driver, were swarthy and wore colorful shirts with big square buttons, round woolen caps with small tassels at their sagging peaks, and wide sashes. Their breeches were tight at the knees and ended in leather leggings laced with yellow thongs.

Dan had seen men like these on westbound trains passing through Yellow Lance. They were Basques, natives of the Spanish-French Pyrénées, heading for Nevada or the valleys of California where big sheep ranchers were in need of such men whose talent for flock-tending was their birthright.

The Basques were hawk-nosed, with dark, proud eyes that fiercely roved doors and windows as they rode by. The stocks of rifles jutted from saddle slings. Pistols and dirks jutted from their sashes.

Dan halted to watch this pageantry pass by. He instantly became the target of three pairs of suspicious eyes. The Basques inspected him briefly, decided that his attention was no more than curiosity, then lost interest in him.

The big wagon swung off the street into a loading lot alongside a rambling supply building near the railroad tracks.

Dan resumed his way to Heather House. As he reached its steps, a woman emerged, accompanied by a small boy. They were in a hurry. The woman was perhaps in her sixties. She wore a duck saddle jacket, and a man's stiff-brimmed range hat was set on her short-cropped, iron-gray hair. Her eyes, steely gray, passed over Dan quickly, measuring him and his luggage, with a glance. He felt that he had been catalogued and filed for possible future reference in that one look.

"Kin I ride back to the basin with André an' the boys, Gran'ma?" the lad was demanding. He looked to be about six years of age.

"Now why would you want to ride sixty miles in a freight wagon, darling?" the woman protested. "My land, you'd have your teeth jolted out."

"I wanna, Gran'ma. I wanna! André said he'd show me how they used to hunt goats in the old country."

"Well, we'll see."

The child had on a duck jacket and hat that were small replicas of those worn by the gray-haired woman. He sported saddle breeches that had been hand-tailored. These were thrust in small saddleboots.

Dan surmised that the lad's clothes, of which he was obviously very proud, were the product of his grandmother's needlework. Her riding skirt, which had been of good quality, was immaculate, but obviously had seen mendings, and was threadbare. Her riding boots had the wrinkles and ease of old friends, and they too had known better days.

Dan watched them hurry down the street to the supply store where the three Basques, now on foot, were waiting. The group chatted for a moment, with the Basques removing their tasseled caps and showing white teeth in smiles. Then the lot of them vanished into the mercantile.

Dan turned to enter the boardinghouse and found a stout, aproned woman in the doorway. She was peering in the direction of the mercantile.

She moved hastily out of Dan's path. "I didn't aim to block the trail," she said amiably. "You lookin' for accommodations? I'm Jenny Heather, the owner."

"Until Friday," Dan said. "They tell me I can't take stage to Flat Butte until then."

"Flat Butte?" Jenny Heather's placid features changed a trifle. He saw in her something of the unasked questions and speculation he had encountered in the agent's manner at the stage station.

"Anything wrong with that?" he asked.

"Wrong? Why, o' course not. I've got a nice pleasant room. A dollar an' four bits a day with meals. We eat mighty well here. You're a cowhand, I take it?"

"That's right," Dan said. "That's cow country down that way, isn't it?"

"So they tell me," said Jenny Heather.

Dan signed the register. "What outfit is that?" he asked, jerking a thumb in the direction of the mercantile.

"The Shannons," the landlady said. She almost sniffed the name. "That was Lavinia Shannon, herself, that you passed. She's stayin' here with her grandson 'til stage time. Came in Monday to buy supplies. The Basques will wagon the stuff back to Springwater Basin."

"I thought you said that was cow country?"

Jenny Heather's face became bland and neutral. "You'll find the washroom at the far end o' the hall, if you want to fresh up before supper, Mr.—Mr.—" she consulted the register. "Mr. Driscoll, isn't it? You forgot to put down where you was from, Mr. Driscoll."

"So I did," Dan said.

She waited, then said hastily, "Tub bath is two bits extry. Most folks could use a little soap an' water after ridin' the old Santy Fee."

Dan was thoughtful as he shaved and scrubbed in the tub. He decided he was self-conscious about his new identity and that the attitude of Jenny Heather and the stagecoach manager had been due only to natural curiosity toward strangers.

He ate supper at the long table in the dining room. More than a dozen others were present. Among them was the stagecoach agent, who selected a chair well away from Dan and made a point of ignoring his presence.

Neither Lavinia Shannon nor her grandson appeared for the meal. Later, as Dan strolled the street in the twilight, he saw the Shannon freight wagon camped on the fringe of town with a cookfire burning. The elderly woman and her grandson were eating with the three Basques, evidently preferring the company of her herders to that of the guests at Jenny Heather's table.

Dan played small limit poker in a saloon for two hours.

He cashed in five dollars to the good, but wandered to a poolroom and lost his winnings to a fat man, who, it turned out, owned the establishment and made the biggest part of his living playing for money.

He finally turned in at his room in Heather House and did not stir until the breakfast gong clanged in the kitchen.

Lavinia Shannon again chose the camp cooking of the Basques for her breakfast, and also the noon meal. It was evident that Jenny Heather's nose was bent by this disdain of her cooking. Dan wondered if this was the real reason for her attitude toward the older woman.

He whiled away the afternoon reading a week-old newspaper and an older magazine in the sitting room of the boardinghouse. Bored with that, he returned to the poolroom and played rotation with the fat man, at four bits a game. The fat man made it plain he did not often waste time on such picayune wagers. He even let Dan win a game or two in an attempt to lure him into hiking the stakes.

The other two tables became busy. Men drifted in to occupy the chairs along the wall while they drank beer, gossiped and watched the play.

The Shannon supply wagon, now heavily laden, rolled past, heading out of town on the trail by which it had arrived the previous day. Little Chad Shannon sat on the seat, bright-eyed and happy. The driver was letting the lad believe he was handling the team, which had grown accustomed to the sight of buildings and was also tamed by the weight of the load in the vehicle.

The driver had a six-shooter in his sash, and a rifle was slung in a scabbard lashed alongside the seat. The two Basques who again were serving as outriders, seemed to make a point of proving they were heavily armed.

Lavinia Shannon stood in front of Heather House, waving and smiling as long as the wagon was in sight. Then she entered the boardinghouse.

The poolroom owner, peering through the window at the departing wagon, said, "Good riddance! Too bad Livvy Shannon didn't go with 'em. I reckon she's got more bank business to clear up an' has to lay over to ride home by stage tomorrow. I hear she's havin' to scratch mighty deep to raise money so as to keep goin'. I say it'll be a happy day when she goes under. I don't cotton to the kind o'

30

Dan watched Alex Emmons enter Heather House, carrying his luggage. A memory came that he wanted to forget. He was seeing Frank Buckman again, young, fair-haired, handsome, the same jaunty stride, the same chip on his shoulder.

"I say ag'in," a man was declaring, "Katey Royal won't never marry nobody, least of all Alex Emmons."

Katey Royal! Dan suddenly became keenly alert to the conversation. However, the poolroom owner changed the subject, and the others seemed glad to drop the matter of the Shannons and Alex Emmons.

Dan finally returned to Heather House. The sitting room was cooler than the street, and he resumed the sleepy task of poring over the reading material.

However, his mind was elsewhere. John Cass had said that the daughter of the owner of Spanish Bell was a widow. From his discussions with Cass, Dan had the impression that Kate Royal was a matronly, middle-aged person, kindly enough, but befuddled by the responsibility of managing a cattle ranch.

Perhaps this Kate Royal the poolroom patrons had been talking about was a daughter of the widow. Certainly, Alex Emmons was palpably not the type to pursue in a romantic way the sort of person Dan had pictured from John Cass's words.

And the Mayor of Yellow Lance had led Dan astray on another matter. There was evidently trouble in Paradise—Springwater Basin in this case. Real trouble, evidently, which divided the opinion of citizens in this town, ninety miles away. Perhaps John Cass had not known of the situation. Dan gave him the benefit of that doubt, at least.

In any event Dan was forewarned. His interest in the matter was now purely academic. Impersonal. But he *was* curious.

Alex Emmons appeared from his room. He was shaved and combed and had changed to more conservative garb. He wore a white shirt with a black string tie and dark trousers. It was a considerable contrast to the attire in which he had arrived. It was calculated to make him appear more mature and steadfast. But he still carried the black-handled six-shooter.

Emmons, of course, was dressed to impress the person he had come to Flag to meet. Kate Royal, if the pool patrons were on the right track. Emmons walked through the sitting room and to the street, giving Dan only a disinterested glance.

The distant wail of a whistle announced the approach of a train from the East. Alex Emmons lengthened his stride as he headed down the street toward the depot.

Dan arose and moved to the window to watch. Within him was disappointment. He had not realized until this moment how high he had built his hopes. It was that name—Springwater Basin—that had deluded him with its picture of peace and a chance to start a new career under a new name.

That was over now, of course. The stage for Flat Butte and Springwater Basin would be leaving in the morning, but he would not be aboard. He had the sudden impulse to hurry to the depot and catch this westbound train, whose destination must be California.

But the whistle of the locomotive was loud over the town. He could hear the slap of couplings and the grind of wheels as the express made its stop. There would be no time to gather his belongings and reach the depot in time.

He relaxed. There was no real need for haste. There would be another train tomorrow. Then he admitted the real reason why he was content to stay a few more hours. He wanted to get a look at this Kate Royal. What was it someone had called her in the poolroom? Her royal highness.

He remained at his viewpoint which commanded the end of the depot where the locomotive and a mail car blocked the street. Passengers carrying luggage began to straggle into view. The engineer was busy with his long-spouted oil-can, like a bee poking into the vitals of his steaming, fuming bouquet of steel.

Alex Emmons came into view, his hand on the arm of a woman. She was obviously slender and tall, but she wore a linen dust coat and had a scarf tied over the top of her bonnet and under her chin so that age, shape, and beauty were impossible to estimate at this distance.

Alex Emmons was being very possessive and very gallant. He escorted his companion to a livery cab which he evidently had reserved, and helped her into its interior. He saw to it that the driver brought baggage from the depot and stored it aboard.

Emmons, after making sure Kate Royal was seated, turned to hurry around the cab to the street side in order to enter the vehicle. He collided violently with a burly bystander who stepped into his path. He was staggered by the force of the impact and began to fall. He escaped sprawling in the dust by grasping a wheel of the cab and hanging to it.

His hat rolled in the dust. He clung ignominiously to the cab wheel. Some of the onlookers began to guffaw.

The man who had caused the mishap stood watching Alex Emmons' discomfiture. This man was not guffawing. He merely stood, short, heavy legs spread slightly apart. Watching. Waiting.

Dan suddenly tensed, staring. The burly man had turned slightly so that his face was visible. Dan recognized him. He was a bulky person, who might be called fat at first glance. This man was not fat. He stood five feet nine, and weighed perhaps two hundred and thirty pounds. He had fought in the ring, using several names under both the bare knuckle and Queensbury rules.

Since Dan had last seen him, Shep Sand had grown a thick black mustache. He had a flattened nose, and a left ear that was a mass of scar tissue. He had been both a professional pugilist and a gunman. He had a reputation as a barroom bruiser where nothing was barred, and opponents could be blinded or maimed for life. As a gunman, for hire, it was said he fought the same way. Mainly from a bushwhack.

Alex Emmons straightened. He was ashen. He knew the collision had been staged in order to bait him into fighting. He had his choice. Fists or the six-shooter at his side. Dan knew Shep Sand was armed, no doubt, although the loose sack coat the man wore in spite of the afternoon heat, concealed any weapon.

What young Emmons probably did not know was that he had no chance either way. He probably had never been called on to draw a weapon in an open duel in his life. As for fists, there could be only one outcome. He would be demolished.

Dan could follow the workings of Emmons' mind. He had faced a situation similar to this when he had been twenty years old. He had preferred probable death rather than humble his pride by backing down to an older opponent with whom he had clashed.

However, there had been a difference. He had not been facing Shep Sand. It was his opponent who had wilted and walked away rather than fight. That was the day Diamond Dan Briscoe had been born. That was the day Dan had learned that the average, self-professed bad man's image was hollow when tested with steel. That was the day he had started building up his reputation.

But Alex Emmons was not up against the average bad man. Shep Sand, whatever he might be, was hard all the way through, and cold. And he was now on the kill. He felt sure his victim's choice would be pistols. Even Alex Emmons must know that he was up against a man he could not handle in a fistfight.

Emmons was not allowed to make the choice. Kate Royal, acting swiftly, leaped from the cab and placed herself between the two men. She said something to Shep Sand, but at that distance Dan could not hear the words.

Alex Emmons had no wish to be protected by skirts. He attempted to push Kate Royal out of his way. He was aghast at this new humiliation.

She would not yield. She wrapped her arms around him, preventing with lithe strength his enraged effort to break away and go for his pistol. Her hat fell back, hanging down her back, caught by the scarf. She had thick hair of a dark chestnut hue, and features that were finely chiseled around large dark-gray eyes that were very angry.

As she held Emmons helpless she spoke again to Shep Sand, words that only she and Sand and Emmons heard, for all bystanders had scattered frantically to cover in fear of wild bullets.

Sand stood there a second or two longer. Then he turned and walked away. Whatever Kate Royal had said had convinced him that this was no longer the time nor the place for what he had come there to do.

Sand came walking past the window of the boardinghouse where Dan still stood. Sand's muddy eyes, set deep beneath heavy brows, settled on Dan for a moment, then discarded him and moved elsewhere. The man entered a saloon farther down the street.

Dan was sure he had not been recognized. In fact, he doubted if Sand had ever seen him, face-to-face. The gunman had never been in Yellow Lance to Dan's knowledge. He had watched Sand fight two bouts, one at Cheyenne, the other at Green River, Wyoming, but he had been only one of the faces in the crowds on those occasions.

Jenny Heather was at Dan's side, peering, her hands nervously twisting her apron. "My good land!" she said weakly. "I was afeared that nice young man was goin' to git himself killed right there in front of Kate Royal's eyes. It's an outrage. That awful Tom Smith ought to be strung up."

"Tom Smith?"

"He's that ugly toad who tried to start the fight. Then he'd claim self-defense, like all them killers do."

"What's he got against that young cowboy?"

"Nothin' 'special. It's Kate Royal he's really after. He's been hangin' around Flag ever since she left fer the East a couple o' weeks ago. He was sent here to wait 'til she got back an' start trouble all over ag'in, I reckon."

"Sent? Who sent him?"

"Why, Livvy—" Jenny Heather decided she was talking too much. "How would I know?" she snapped. She started to turn away.

Dan had another question. "Where is Kate Royal's mother?"

Jenny Heather stared, mouth agape. "Katey's mother? You mean Nancy Royal? Why, Nancy's been dead for years. She died when Katey was only a little girl. That was more'n twenty years ago. Katey's, let's see, why she must be twenty-six or -seven now."

Dan let Jenny Heather escape to the kitchen. John Cass *had* given him the wrong impression of events and people in Springwater Basin.

Dan felt great compassion for Alex Emmons. And pity. He believed that Emmons did not have long to live.

CHAPTER FOUR

Alex Emmons and Kate Royal entered the hansom and were driven down the street to some destination westward. The train pulled out. The sun-baked street became almost deserted. The heads and faces that had appeared at doors and windows during the clash, had popped out of sight again.

Dan had another night to put in before he could leave this place and its feuds. He suddenly felt forlorn, without purpose in life. Again he realized how really high he had built his dreams of Springwater Basin.

John Cass, of course, certainly had deceived him. He had been led to the mountain and had been offered a vision of everything he desired—peace and forgetfulness, when the truth was there seemed to be only hatred and strife in the range John Cass had pictured as a place of contentment and opportunity.

He walked to the depot. The ticket agent, who was preparing to close up the office for a few hours, told him there would not be a through train to California until ten o'clock the next morning.

"I hear there's a big cattle outfit in California called Miller and Lux," Dan said. "Just where would a man go to see their foreman about a job?"

The agent laughed. "Most anywhere along about three hundred miles, from Bakersfield, California, to Reno, Nevada, from what I'm told. If it was me, I'd buy fare to Bakersfield, then start ridin' the grub line. They say the M. and L. cooks has orders to feed everybody what comes through. Henry Miller figures it's good insurance ag'in saddle bums helpin' themselves to free beef."

This was the future the man was seeing for Dan. Drifting. Riding forever, being fed and passed along from ranch to ranch, from cow camp to cow camp, bribed with free meals against helping himself to cattle or horses.

For want of anything else to do, Dan returned to the poolroom. All tables were active. He took a spectator's chair. He expected that the clash between Alex Emmons and the pseudo Tom Smith would be a live object of conversation. He was wrong. What talk there was steered so wide of the subject that he understood it was being carefully avoided.

He returned to Heather House when the supper gong sounded. There were three new guests at the table, but neither Kate Royal nor Alex Emmons was present.

Later, after darkness had come, he was sitting in one of the chairs that he and half a dozen others had carried to the sidewalk to take advantage of the cooling evening breeze. He was smoking a cigarette when Alex Emmons came striding past and entered the boardinghouse.

Emmons was obviously steaming with anger. He took the steps to the door three at a time and stamped inside. He was unarmed. His black holster and gun were missing. Dan believed he had the answer. Kate Royal probably had seen to it that the young, hot-headed cowboy had shed his six-shooter, fearing he would hunt up Shep Sand.

Approval stirred in Dan. What few cattle women he had encountered in the past had been of the leathery, brassy type who drank their whiskey straight and had been made rough and mannish by hardship and environment. Apparently, Kate Royal was cut from a different bolt of cloth. Fine silk instead of rough burlap.

Dan finally arose and strolled down the street, heading for a gambling house named the Big Chance, whose lights were brighter than its competitors. He had in mind the thought of buying chips in a modest-limit stud poker game in order to while away the evening.

Only the monte table was in operation. The shirt-sleeved house dealer, wearing celluloid eyeshade and black sleeve supporters, was waiting to flip a card to one of the two players. This man wore a loose dark sack coat and a white linen shirt with a stiff starched collar, adorned with a plaid bow tie. He chewed a toothpick as he studied his two cards. He had a hard, bony face whose structure seemed two sizes small for his wrinkled skin. An old, white scar crossed the wrinkles from cheekbone to the line of the jaw.

Dan had never before set eyes on Gideon Marko, but the toothpick and the scar were enough. These characteristics had been described to him and to other law officers by word of mouth and, at times, on lists of wanted men.

The other man at the table was the heavy-shouldered Shep Sand. Dan recalled that the information law officers passed along to each other had mentioned that Gid Marko and Shep Sand usually operated together.

The presence of the pair at the monte table apparently had put a damper on business, for no other games were open. The bar was deserted.

Dan ordered a glass of beer at the bar, and stood there, sipping it. He had been aware of the way Shep Sand and Gid Marko reacted when he had entered. They were sitting so that Sand faced the front door and Marko the only other entrance which was at the side and to the rear. The small windows, set high in the walls, were blanked out by dusty shades.

Both men had shifted ever so slightly when Dan had stepped through the door. The dealer had braced himself so as to be ready to seek safety. Sand and Marko had been expecting someone. Expecting trouble.

Dan watched their reflections in the back bar mirror. They had lost interest in him. That satisfied him that Gid Marko, like his companion, did not know that he had been the marshal of wild Yellow Lance.

Who were they expecting? Dan suddenly had the probable answer. Alex Emmons. Somehow, that jolted him. He finished his beer, tossed a coin on the bar and said, "That'll hold me for a little while."

He walked out of the place. And just in time to see Alex Emmons emerging from Heather House down the street. His hunch had been right. Emmons was armed now. He was carrying a six-shooter in a much-used leather holster. The gun was the commonplace, inexpensive weapon that a rider would carry with him on the range. Evidently Emmons had brought this gun with him in his saddle pouch to fall back on in case of need.

Dan melted into the shelter of a dark recessed doorway in a store building next to the saloon. Emmons crossed the street, heading directly for the Big Chance. Striding to his death. Driven by pride. Bent on making up for his humiliation in the presence of Kate Royal.

Emmons was not aware Dan stood in the dark doorway. He had eyes only for the lighted entrance to the Big Chance. In the glow of that light Dan could see the bloodless set of Emmons' face. Alex Emmons knew these might be the last moments of his life.

What Dan did then was the last thing in the world he had in mind. Something drove him to intervene in an affair in which he had no stake.

He stepped silently from the doorway, a stride back of Alex Emmons and drove his clenched fist to the side of the neck below the ear. It was a blow that had been taught him by Wyatt Earp, who had won fame as a law man in Dodge City and Tombstone. Their paths had happened to cross when Dan had been a young, eager deputy in Cheyenne.

"Better to beef 'em than shoot 'em," Wyatt Earp had said. "Right below the ear. It paralyzes nerves and muscles. Aim it just a little toward the spinal cord. But be careful. You can kill a man if you swing too hard."

Alex Emmons staggered blindly. He made a reflex motion toward his six-shooter, which failed. Dan caught him before he went down, and backed into the doorway with his burden sagging in his arms.

He peered out. With one exception, his interference in Emmons' purpose had escaped notice. A figure loomed at arm's length.

"Don't you dare move!" a feminine voice breathed. "I've got a pistol, and I'll shoot if you try to kill him."

She was Kate Royal. "Don't be a fool!" Dan snorted. "He isn't hurt! He's only knocked out. Get in here off the sidewalk before somebody sees you. Your friend here will be almost as good as new in about ten minutes."

Kate Royal moved closer, peering at Dan's face in the faint light. "Oh!" she murmured. She seemed shocked into silence for a space.

Footsteps were approaching on the sidewalk. She moved into the doorway, pressing against Dan and the stunned burden he held. Two men walked past, smoking, and failed to notice that the door was occupied.

"You—you're sure he's not hurt?" she whispered.

"Of course he's hurt," Dan growled. "He might even have a broken jaw. I hope not. But he won't enjoy chewing his grub for a day or two, at best."

"Why did you hit him?" she asked.

"I wish I knew," Dan snarled.

"He was going into that saloon to start trouble with a gunman," she said. "You knew that, didn't you?"

"Lady, do you try to read everybody's mind?"

"But, I don't understand. Why did you—?"

"For pete's sake, Lady, I don't know why I stopped him. Just a busybody, maybe. I ought to know better. But we can't stay here, powwowing. We better get him away from here."

"I've got a carriage handy," she whispered. "It'll only take a minute or two. Pretend he's drunk and that you're helping him in case somebody sees you. Who are you?"

"Just a cowboy passing through town," Dan said.

"What's your name?"

"Driscoll!" Dan snapped impatiently. "Now, will you please—!"

"I'll hurry!" she said, and was gone.

Alex Emmons began to mumble and stir. Dan sat him in a dark corner and hovered over him. What he feared was that Shep Sand or Marko might come out of the saloon and become inquisitive. A passerby discovered them, slowed his pace, and peered. But the man went about his business when Dan, pretending he was also fortified with spirits, mumbled that he needed no help in taking care of his old riding pal.

A top buggy pulled up. It was driven by Kate Royal. She was hatless, but had a scarf tied over her hair. Dan now also saw that she wore a white, open-throated shirtwaist and a dark skirt. Gold earrings dangled. He had the impression that she must have hurriedly left a supper party.

"I'm staying with friends at their home on the edge of town," she breathed, alighting from the rig. "This is their carriage. We'll take Alex there."

Dan lifted Alex Emmons onto the seat of the buggy. Kate Royal helped stuff his limp legs into place. She squeezed herself into the driver's seat.

"Glad to be of help," Dan said, standing back.

"Oh, but you've got to come with me!" she exclaimed. "You must. I can't handle him alone. What if he wakes up?"

More pedestrians were approaching. "All right," Dan said reluctantly. He crowded into the carriage, with the dazed Alex Emmons between them. Emmons was groaning and beginning to fight his way back to the surface.

The buggy lurched into motion as Kate Royal flicked the whip. As they passed the door of the Big Chance, Dan glimpsed Shep Sand in the parted swing portals, peering up and down the sidewalk.

Kate Royal saw this also. "The fool!" she said, and choked up a trifle.

"Who? The one back there?"

"No. This one here with us. Conceit is a terrible thing." She looked down at Alex Emmons. Tenderness came into her voice. "And sometimes it's wonderful too."

She looked at Dan. "Alex might not appreciate what you did for him, but I do. I want to thank you, Mr.—Mr.— was the name Driscoll?"

"That's it," Dan said. "Daniel Driscoll."

"People in these parts usually don't want to get involved in—in—" She didn't finish it, letting it hang in the air.

When Dan didn't help her out by asking what she meant, she spoke again. "You must have seen what happened at the depot this afternoon. You knew Alex was going to that saloon to have it out with that man, Tom Smith."

"Maybe," Dan said.

"I still don't understand why you stopped him, Mr. Driscoll."

"Maybe I figured he was too young to die."

She was silent for a time. She finally drew a long, quivering breath. "Yes," she said huskily. "Oh, yes."

"How come you showed up there at that moment?" Dan asked.

"After the trouble at the depot I managed to talk Alex into going to the house where I'm staying overnight with old friends, Ed and Ann Davis. I insisted that he leave with me that awful, show-off gun he had been carrying. He stayed for supper, and I had believed he had cooled off. After he left, I became afraid he'd do exactly what he tried to do. Bill Davis had hitched up his buggy, for he was to attend his lodge meeting tonight. I didn't have time to explain. I borrowed it and headed for town. I saw Alex walking toward the Big Chance and saw you slug him."

She added, "I was going to do just what you did. You beat me to it."

"What? You were going to slug him? With what?"

"Well, not with a fist, of course. I've got a Colt .44. I intended to use that on his stubborn skull."

"Emmons was lucky I happened to be around," Dan said. "He's coming around already. You might have laid him out for quite a spell. The barrel of a six-gun can do a lot of damage."

"Better a broken head than a grave," she said. "Well, here we are, Mr. Driscoll."

She had swung the buggy into the driveway of a modest dwelling. Windows were lighted. Alex Emmons' eyes were open, the pupils rolling weakly. Dan alighted. With Kate Royal's help, he lifted Emmons from the vehicle and stood him on his feet. Supporting him between them they helped him to the house.

The door was opened by a comely young matron. "Good heavens!" she exclaimed. "Where did you go, Kathleen? What happened?"

"Nothing too serious, Ann," Kate Royal said. "Alex got punched in the jaw. This is his day to lose all the fights."

Ann Davis's husband came hurrying. Dan handed his share of the burden over to him, and turned to leave.

"Wait!" Kate Royal cried. "Please!"

Dan halted reluctantly and waited while Alex Emmons was led off to a bedroom. Ann Davis prepared cold cloths in the kitchen, and she and Kate Royal bustled about, debating the merits of liniment and other medication.

Ed Davis introduced himself to Dan. "You're new around here?" he asked.

"Name is Dan Driscoll," Dan said. "I'm just stopping over for a day or two. Heading for California."

"What happened?"

"I sort of got mixed in by accident," Dan said. "I don't know exactly what all this is about. I reckon the young lady can tell you better than I can."

"Young lady?"

"Her name's Royal, I believe. That's the one I mean."

"You don't even know who she is? Kate Royal?"

"Only by hearsay."

Kate Royal returned at that moment. "Alex will be all right," she said. "Not even a broken jaw. You probably saved his life, Mr. Driscoll."

"I'll be saying good night, then," Dan said.

"Are you looking for a riding job?" she asked quickly.

"I reckon not," Dan said. "I'm moving farther west in the morning."

"We could offer you a steady job," she said. She was removing the dangling earrings. She kneaded the lobes of her ears and said, "I should never wear those things. They're brutally heavy. But they're beautiful. Heirlooms."

She added, "My father owns a ranch down in the Springwater. That's south of here. Some of the range is rough country, no question about that. We pay forty a month to a rider who isn't afraid of popping cattle in the brush and on the slants. Fifty a month for roundup work. We're not bothered much with fence scars nor heelfly down there. Some ticks, of course, but only in early summer. We mount our men on good horseflesh. Quarterhorse stock."

"Sorry, ma'am—" Dan mumbled.

But she continued with her sales pitch. "We furnish good grub. Fact is, I do most of the cooking myself. I know you'd like the country."

Dan burst into a grin. She smiled also. "Have I convinced you?" she asked.

"Sorry," Dan said. "It sounds like a cowpuncher's dream of the ranch in the sky. But I'm pulling out tomorrow."

Her forced animation faded. She tried to hide her disappointment, but Dan saw that it was very bitter to her. That puzzled him.

"I can't blame you," she said tiredly. It was as though she had reached a dead end on some mental road, and had no immediate plan for finding her way onward.

Dan had heard Ann Davis address her as "Kathleen." He felt that suited her better than the abbreviated "Kate."

He said again, "I'm sorry. I'll say good night now."

She extended a hand. "Good night, Mr. Driscoll. And thanks again for what you did. I'll always—"

The earrings she had been holding slipped from her hand and rolled on the carpet at Dan's feet. Instinctively, they both stooped to retrieve them. Their heads collided. Dan caught Kathleen Royal's arm to prevent her from toppling.

They steadied themselves and straightened, laughing shakily. "My fault," Dan said. "I hope you aren't hurt."

"Not at all," she said. She had gripped his arm in order to support herself, and she continued to cling for a moment or two. She was still swaying, and leaned against him for an instant. She laughed again, and said, "I'm all right now. How awkward of me."

Dan looked down. "The earrings?" he asked.

"Never mind," she said. "I'll find the other one later. I have one."

"Good night," Dan said. "Good night, Mr. and Mrs. Davis. It's been a real pleasure."

He left Kathleen Royal standing in the doorway, outlined by the lamplight as he walked away. Again he felt there was in her a disappointment that amounted to despair. He carried with him a sense of guilt. It was as

45

though she felt he had betrayed a confidence, ended some last hope within her.

He found himself entering the one place his instinct told him to avoid. The Big Chance saloon. But Shep Sand and Gideon Marko had left the place. Other players were at the monte table. A poker game was in operation. The stakes seemed about the modest size Dan was in the mood to play. He was told it was an open game and there was a vacant chair. He sat in.

There was nothing professional in the play of his opponents. His luck was average. At one time he was fifteen dollars or so in the hole. An hour later he was a few dollars ahead.

They dealt the last hand at eleven o'clock. He was exactly two dollars to the good when he cashed in his chips. He bought a round of drinks with his winnings, and shook hands all around.

It had been a convivial game, and he had won friends. It was the first time he had enjoyed his change of identity. He knew how it would have been if they had been aware they were playing with Diamond Dan Briscoe. There would have been no warmth, no pleasure in the game. They would have been tense and either overaggressive, or too anxious to avoid opposing him.

He left the Big Chance and strolled the sidewalk, delaying his return to Heather House. The night was clear and refreshing. The Milky Way was a luminous cloud in the sky. The town slept, with few lights burning. Sounds traveled far.

He reached the west limit of the plank sidewalk and started to turn back. He pulled up. Two riders came out of the starlight ahead and passed by at a trot.

One was Kathleen Royal. With her was Alex Emmons. She saw Dan standing on the sidewalk, but made no sign of recognition. Alex Emmons must have seen him also, but did not give him a second glance. There was no way for Emmons to know that Dan was the man who had slugged him.

They swung off the street, taking the wagon trail out of town that headed southward. The hoofbeats faded into the night. The town became silent again.

Apparently, Kathleen Royal had decided it was best to get Alex Emmons out of Flag before he could force another encounter with Shep Sand. There went, Dan told himself, a person in deep trouble. Apparently it was gun trouble. Of that he wanted no part.

Still, within him, the emptiness deepened. He would always remember the lithe grace and womanliness of Kathleen Royal, the richness of her hair, the slenderness of her hands. Above all, he would never forget the depths of despair and hopelessness that had shadowed her eyes. Again the guilt came back in his mind. He angrily tried to dismiss that. He owed no one in this new country anything, least of all Kathleen Royal.

He entered Heather House, but was still in no mood for sleep. The sitting room was dark and deserted, all lamps having been turned out with the exception of one that burned low back of the clerk's counter.

He took one of the lumpy, stuffed, leather-bound chairs, and sat in the semidarkness, looking out into Flag's sleeping street, smoking one cigarette after another.

He became aware he was not entirely alone. A silent figure occupied a similar chair in the farthest corner. Like himself, this guest had preferred the sitting room to the confinement of a bedroom until the desire to sleep came.

The other person was Lavinia Shannon, the gray-haired grandmother. She arose to go to her room. She paused abruptly, looking down at him. "What does it take to bring wolves like you to the kill?" she demanded.

Dan got to his feet, amazed. "Ma'am?"

"Not blood," Lavinia Shannon went on. "Blood doesn't feed human wolves. It has to be money. Well, I've got money, too. I'll double any offer Kate Royal has made to you."

"I don't know what you're talking about," Dan said. But he did know.

"You've got an oily tongue," Lavinia Shannon said. "A person would almost believe you. But I saw you riding in the carriage with her. With Kate Royal. And with that lovesick young cowboy who wants to marry her."

She turned away and said, over her shoulder, "You're one of them. She brought you here. Gun scum!"

She moved down the hall toward her quarters. A night lamp burned down the hall. Lavinia Shannon's silhouette was as straight as that of a young woman. She must have been a raving beauty in the fullness of her days. She was still a strikingly attractive personality, stamped with the hallmark of an indomitable spirit.

Gun scum! She had classified him with Shep Sand and Gid Marko. A killer for pay. She had seen him in the carriage with Kathleen Royal and Alex Emmons, but evidently had not witnessed what had happened previously. She believed he had been imported by Kathleen Royal as a fighting man. But he doubted that she knew his real identity. He felt that if that were so, she would have mentioned it.

That drove sleep from him for another hour. The stubs of half-burned cigarettes filled the ashtray. The contempt in Lavinia Shannon's voice kept roweling him. He wondered how much greater her scorn might have been if she had known that he was Diamond Dan Briscoe.

He finally went to his room and prepared to turn in. As he removed his shirt a small object fell from the breast pocket from which he had removed his sack of cigarette tobacco. It lay at his feet, shining dully in the lamplight.

It was one of the earrings Kathleen Royal had worn. He picked it up. The pendant was in the shape of a tiny Spanish bell. It was of gold, and exquisitely made. It even had a tiny clapper which tinkled with elfin music.

He dangled it in his hand, torn between grim amusement and irritation. An heirloom, she had said. Treasured by her, no doubt. It had not been placed in his pocket by accident. She had dropped the ornament there as she had clung to him during that moment of confusion when their heads had collided at the Davis home. She had engineered the whole thing from the moment she had dropped the earrings on purpose.

And that purpose was self-evident. She meant to obligate him into making the trip to Flat Butte. She was trying to override his refusal of her offer of a riding job with the Spanish Bell crew.

He hefted the ornament in his hand. The arrogance of her! She had a woman's privilege, of course, of pretending that this was meant as an indication that she might have more than a passing interest in him, and wanted to further their acquaintanceship.

But he knew that she had much more in mind. He placed the earring in his wallet, blew out the lamp and got into bed. He wanted no part of Kathleen Royal, or of

Springwater Basin and its deep waters. As sleep still eluded him, he kept assuring himself he was not being lured into further involvement in whatever was brewing. He was catching the westbound Santa Fe express in the morning.

As for the earring, he would turn it over to her friends, the Davis couple, and let them deliver it to its owner.

Each time that was finally decided in his mind, the memory of Lavinia Shannon would return, and he would hear her voice saying, "Gun scum!"

Lavinia Shannon was being unfair. Surely, those three years at Yellow Lance hadn't put *that* brand indelibly on him. The brand that men like Shep Sand and Gideon Marko wore. The stain of brutality and indifference to human life.

He regretted he had failed to explain to Lavinia Shannon that she had misjudged him. He promised himself he would do so in the morning.

Then he realized it was not only Lavinia Shannon he had in mind. It was also Kathleen Royal he was thinking about, and wanted to see again.

CHAPTER FIVE

Dan was at the door of the dining room when it opened for breakfast at sunrise. However, Lavinia Shannon did not come to the table, evidently having had her morning meal taken to her room.

The stagecoach came jostling to the door of Heather House fifteen minutes before departure time, for the majority of its fares were breakfasting there. Mail sacks bulged the boot and a few were lashed to the roof.

Dan ate glumly. "This is ridiculous," he kept telling himself. "What do I care what Lavinia Shannon thinks of me? I'll never see her again after this morning."

"Five minutes, folks," the coach driver shouted, pouring syrup on the last of the flapjacks a waitress had brought for him. "Cedar Ford, 'Pache Rock, Goldstone, Flat Butte, Mogollon, an' all points beyond as fur as Prescott."

There were three other fares finishing the meal. Lavinia

Shannon appeared, wearing a dust coat, with a veil ready for use on her hat. A handyman carried her carpetbag.

Dan arose, intending to speak to her, but he was chilled by her eyes, hostile as gun bores. She walked past, drawing her skirt aside as though to avoid contamination.

He took a stride to halt her. She had to give him a hearing. But, he realized that this was not the time or the place, with so many around to eavesdrop.

He watched her board the stage. No hand was lifted to assist her. He sensed that such an offer would have been scorned if it had been made. However, all other passengers stood back, waiting for Lavinia Shannon to select the seat she preferred. At least they respected her. More likely, Dan reflected, it was fear of her.

He suddenly reached an unexpected decision, as abrupt as the one he had made when he had intervened to prevent Alex Emmons from throwing away his life.

"Hold up until I get my possibles," he said to the driver. "I've decided to buy fare with you today."

"Whar to?"

"Flat Butte," Dan said.

Within a few minutes he was seated opposite Lavinia Shannon, clinging to a swing strap, as the stage bucked the chuckholes out of town. She continued to ignore his existence.

Sitting alongside her were two passengers Dan had not counted on. They must have boarded the coach at the stage station before it moved to Heather House. Shep Sand and Gideon Marko. The fifth passenger, who sat with Dan in the forward seat, was palpably a salesman, and did not count.

Lavinia Shannon made no sign that she was acquainted with the two gunmen, or was even aware of their presence. They were equally careful to act as though she was not there. Dan decided that the three of them were too obvious about it. No doubt Sand and Marko had Livvy Shannon's pay in their pockets and probably were awaiting her orders as to their next move, now that Alex Emmons remained alive.

His fingers touched the earring in his pocket to make sure it was still there. A cynical anticipation burned in him. He admitted to himself that he was being theatrical in making the stage trip to Flat Butte in order to return the ornament. He assured himself it was mainly curiosity that had prevailed on him to pretend to take the bait she was offering—along with the deadly hook that probably went with it.

He wondered just how far she would go to win in the apparent feud she had with Lavinia Shannon. And how far would Lavinia Shannon go? Kathleen Royal's shapely attractiveness had nothing to do with his decision. At least that was what he kept telling himself.

He was aware he was being covertly studied by Shep Sand and Gid Marko. They evidently recalled that he had entered the Big Chance the previous evening and had left suddenly. His sudden decision to buy fare to Flat Butte had made him an object of speculation—and suspicion.

He watched them from semiclosed eyes as he pretended to settle into the state of inanimation that was the only defense against the discomforts of travel in a fast-moving coach over rough roads. He believed that their distrust was finally lulled and they had catalogued him as what he really wanted to be—a drifter in search of a riding job.

He felt sure it was much different with Lavinia Shannon. She had drawn the veil over her face as a protection against dust, so that she could watch without betraying her attention. She sat straight and prim, a gloved hand gripping a swing strap. She had decided he was a hired gunman—hired by Kathleen Royal—but evidently she had not imparted that knowledge to Sand and Marko as yet.

Dan intended to let her know she was wrong and that his visit to Flat Butte would be short. However, the chance did not come, for she avoided him whenever they alighted at the swing stations and roadhouses for meals and change of horses.

The coach carried them deeper into a country that grew increasingly wild and up-ended. Dense pine forests blackened the flanks of the ridges, and, for long stretches, enclosed the road so that it was a mere tunnel through the greenery. Brush masked the mouths of draws and ravines and grew thickly along the occasional rushing streams the horses forded.

What few cattle Dan glimpsed were lean, powerful animals that were running like deer for cover in the thickets. Few of them wore brands. They were mainly old mosshorn mavericks that had outwitted many a roundup. Deer were plentiful, and a band of elk had left mud churned at one of the fords, but had reached cover before the stage rounded into view. Wild turkey foraged for grasshoppers in the clearings.

The country began to open during the afternoon. Meadows broke the monotony of the forest. Occasionally, Dan glimpsed still more open flats southward and at lower elevation.

A rider who was evidently working a brushy draw for cattle, appeared, then vanished. Dan judged that his horse was of quarterhorse breeding, and he believed the brand was in the shape of a bell, though he could not be sure at that distance. The rider straddled a double-rigged saddle that was reinforced by breech and breast straps—the rigging of a brush popper who risked neck and limb in tangled country.

Sundown came, and purple twilight gathered in the draws. Darkness settled. The trail leveled. Dan saw the outline of buttes and ridges against a turquoise sky. It was a surprisingly big country, this Springwater Basin—a wild land. And evidently rich in water and grass. It had the clean smell of pines, of growing grass, of flowing water.

The coach creaked over a gentler trail. The lights of a settlement lifted ahead. Beyond it loomed a massive butte with a top as flat as a table.

"Flat Butte!" the driver called joyfully, for this was the finish of his day's work. "An hour to eat an' wash up for such of you as air bound fer points beyond. You'll have a new driver tonight."

They had lost the salesman at a way point along the route, but had picked up three more fares, all of whom were bound for destinations beyond Springwater Basin.

The coach halted at a livery yard in town, which also served as a swing station for the stage line. Dan alighted and turned to assist Lavinia Shannon. She was numbed by weariness, and automatically accepted his help before she realized who had offered it. She leaned on his arm until she had steadied.

Then she straightened sharply and drew away from him. He was aware of the fierce regret that she had shown the need of aid from anyone, even momentarily, and least of all from him.

"Thank you!" she said icily. She turned away, drawing

the veil from her face, and waited to see that her luggage was unloaded from the boot.

A tall man came hurrying. "Mother!" He kissed Lavinia Shannon, picked up her luggage and led her to a spring-seated ranch wagon that had a team in harness.

"Chad's riding home on the wagon, Heber," Lavinia Shannon said. "I know I shouldn't have given in, but I just couldn't refuse. They ought to pull into the ranch tomorrow night. I saw where the wagon had turned off at Flat Creek to take the butte trail. They'll save miles in this dry weather."

The tall man, who carried a gun in a holster, helped her into the wagon, and they drove out of town southward.

Dan gazed around. The station, with its corrals and barn, stood at the fringe of town, which consisted of a score of buildings. There were two saloons. One had a sign over the sidewalk, Mack's Place. The other was built of whitewashed adobe, with its name lettered on a wall, El Cantina.

"Rooms an' grub at Sim Ricker's fleabag," the driver said, as he handed out baggage.

He was indicating a frame-built hotel down the street. A blacksmith shop nearby had lanterns glinting, and a hammer kept banging on metal as late repairs were being made on a freight wagon. The tired stage team tramped by, traces dragging, heading for water and feed, with a hostler in charge.

The most pretentious structure on the dusty street was a rambling building, constructed of planks and bats, with a tarpaper roof. It had a wide false front on which was painted in big white letters the information that this was the *GREAT SOUTHWESTERN MERCANTILE.*

Dan debated as to whether the saloons might provide a better source of information than the store. He chose the store which was still lighted and open for business.

Carrying his belongings, he crossed the street and entered the mercantile. Closing time evidently was near, for there were no customers and the only person present was an enormous man with an unruly thatch of hay-colored hair who was seated at a high desk, penning entries in a ledger.

This man looked up when Dan's footsteps sounded, laid aside the pen and slid from the high stool. He wore a collarless blue shirt and bib overalls, and had a double chin.

He peered at Dan in the lamplight. "Evenin'!" he boomed. "An' welcome, stranger. You must have got off the stage just now. Welcome to Flat Butte! She ain't much to look at right now, but wait'll she gits goin'."

He thrust a big hand over the counter. Dan, a little taken aback by the warmth of the greeting, found his hand clamped in powerful strength and pumped vigorously.

"Me, I'm Obediah Willit, owner o' the Flat Butte Great Southwestern Mercantile," the big man said. "Offerin' everything needed for the comfort an' prosperity of man an' the health of beasts. From diapers fer the new-born to corn likker for them that needs to warm their bones on cold mornin's. From horse collars to horseplay. Married four times. Buried four wives, bless their souls. Fourteen children, an' forty-two grandchildren. What kin I do for you, Mr.—Mr.—?"

Dan grinned. "Driscoll is the name. Can't say I'm in the market for either diapers or horse collars at the moment, but—"

"Give us time," Obediah Willit thundered. "Springwater Basin is brimmin' with purty gals, waitin' a likely man to marry up with, an' raise a family. I'll see to it that you meet some to look over."

"Sounds like I better keep goin' south on that stage before I get roped, throwed, hog-tied an' branded," Dan said.

The store owner guffawed, leaned across the counter and slapped him on the back. It was a blow meant to stagger him. Dan felt the strength of the beefy hand, but managed to brace himself and show no sign it was anything out of the ordinary.

Willit's curling brows pinched together. He was somewhat chagrined by his failure to impress him.

"There does happen to be one young lady I want to get in touch with," Dan said. "Her name is Kathleen Royal."

Obediah Willit was wide-eyed. "Katey Royal? You know her?"

"Only slightly. Miss Royal left Flag late last night, saddleback, with a friend. I figured the stage would overtake them today, but it seems they rode on through."

Willit nodded. "They pulled in an hour or so ago. Alex Emmons was with her. He went up to Flag by stage to meet her an' side her back. Katey hates stagecoaches. Alex rode with her, horseback, to Flag a couple weeks ago to see her off on the train for the east. Left the horses there, while Alex came back by stage to take care o' things at the ranch."

"She's here?" Dan asked. "In Flat Butte?"

"Nope. They went on out to Royal House. Both of 'em was plumb wore out after sixty miles in the saddle, with only a couple hours rest at the Turkey Crick roadhouse. I don't know why Katey was in such a hurry to git home."

"Royal House?"

"Man, you really air a stranger in these parts. I figured everybody in Arizona had heard o' Royal House. It's head-quarters of Spanish Bell, which grazes stock on more'n half o' the basin. Royal House is only five miles out, not far off the south fork o' the stage trail."

Willit showed disappointment when he could read nothing from Dan's expression. "Air you in such a hurry to see Katey thet you aim to go out there tonight?" he asked.

"No," Dan said. "It'll wait until morning."

"Just what is it thet'll wait?" Willit inquired.

"She lost a piece of jewelry in Flag," Dan said. "I happened to find it. Being as I was heading in this direction I thought I'd fetch it to her personally."

"That's mighty kind o' you," Willit said. "Katey will be grateful."

"I was told I'd find lodging and board at the hotel."

"Sim ought to be able to fix you up. Sim Ricker's his name. Runs the shebang. If he happens to be filled up, come on back. I got a bunk in the storeroom where I can put you up for the night."

Obediah Willit again extended a big, enthusiastic hand. "Most folk around here call me Big Obie," he said. "If you're still around, come Sunday, show up at the meetin' house. I do some preachin' to help out the parson."

"I'll keep that in mind," Dan said.

Dan rented a room for the night at Sim Ricker's hotel. "Reckon you'll want to muck the dust off you," Ricker said. "Cy Keeler's barbershop stays open stage nights to ac-commodate folks like you. He's got hot water an' tubs for a quarter. I saw you go into Obie's store. You a friend o' his?"

"I reckon," Dan said, remembering the handshakes.

"Everybody is. Obie Willit is salt o' the earth. He'd do anything to help you. In the ten years he's been in the basin he's done mighty well. Got a smart head for business, don't fool yourself. We needed a store like the one he's built. We used to have to send to Flag fer most things."

Ricker added, aggrieved, "But there's some that wagon their supplies from Flag rather than do business here in Flat Butte." It was evident he was speaking of Lavinia Shannon.

Dan's room was small, but neat enough, with the customary bed, bureau, washstand, chair and rag rug. He got out a clean shirt and underwear. When he returned to the street to head for the barbershop he saw that Obie Willit's mercantile was closed.

He passed by the open doors of the two saloons. Mack's Place had one patron. In the other, the bartender was knocking pool balls around on a seedy table at the rear. There was no one else in the place.

The clatter of dishes echoed from the dining room at Sim Ricker's hotel. There was little other sign of life in Flat Butte, although the hour was still early. As Dan folded his long legs in the sheet-iron tub and enjoyed the feel of clean water, one discordant thought kept intruding. What had happened to Shep Sand and Gideon Marko? They had dropped out of sight since alighting from the stage.

He mentioned it casually as he paid the barber for a shave and use of the tub. "That heavy-set man and his friend who came in on the stage? We were talking about maybe playin' a little poker tonight. But, I can't locate 'em."

The barber didn't answer for a space during which he gave Dan a second look. He calculated his answer. "You mean Tom Smith an' that Jim Martin feller," he said. "I can't rightly say where they went. Out to their claims, most likely."

"Claims? They're miners?"

"Nope. Homesteaders. Leastwise that's what they call theirselves."

"What do other people call them?"

The barber decided to be careful. "I'll be closin' shop now, friend," he said. "Looks like we might have a thunderstorm before mornin'. We could stand it. Been hot an' dry lately."

Dan spent more than an hour rolling five-card dice at Mack's Place at two bits a game, with Mack as his opponent. As he pushed the leather cup aside after deciding he'd had enough, he said idly, "Just what sort of crops would a sod-buster raise in these parts?"

Mack was helping himself to a stein of beer at the bar spigot. He carefully scraped away the foam and took a deep draught. "You aim to join them homesteaders on the river?" he asked without looking directly at Dan.

"Depends. Just what *do* they raise?"

"Now that's a good question, mister. You reap what you sow, so the Good Book says."

Dan eyed him. "Does anybody in these parts ever give a direct answer to a question?"

"Depends on who does the askin'," Mack responded. "*Buenas noches,* friend. I'm closin' up now."

The lights went out in Mack's Place by the time Dan had crossed the street on his way to the hotel. Just as they had gone out in the barbershop, just as they had been dimmed in Obie Willit's store after his departure.

El Cantina was still lighted. Dan thought of going there to try out the pool table. He decided against it. "Why close the whole blasted town up," he told himself whimsically.

He braced the back of the chair under the knob of the door, before turning in. He felt a trifle foolish, childish. But, somehow, he slept sounder because of that added protection against intruders who never came.

CHAPTER SIX

After breakfast the next morning, Dan walked to the livery. The hostler, who was the usual unshaven, unwashed taciturn type, grunted an assent when he asked if a mount was available for the day.

The animal the man saddled had the short-coupled, powerful build of a well-bred quarterhorse. It bore the Spanish Bell brand. That same iron was stamped on the skirt of the saddle.

Dan's brows lifted. "This stable own this steed?" he asked.

"Course not," the hostler sniffed. "Emilio Sandez brung that hawss in from Spanish Bell late last night. Katey Royal sent word that if a long-coupled gent about your size comes along, lookin' fer a hawss, to give him this one. Yore name's Driscoll, ain't it? Leastways that's what you signed on the register at Sim Ricker's hotel."

"News gets around," Dan said. "And who is Emilio Sandez?"

"Rides fer Spanish Bell," the hostler said. "Anyway, he still was on their payroll last night."

Dan wondered if there had been any significance in that last statement, as he mounted and rode out of town.

"Walk into my parlor, said the spider to the fly," he commented to the horse. "The path is being made easy for me."

The earring was in his pocket. He found himself rather enjoying this game of cat and mouse.

The trail carried him southward through scattered stands of pines. There were open flats that offered fine grazing. He sighted steers with the Bell brand. They were whitefaces and were palpably ready for market. They would only put on unnecessary fat the longer roundup and shipping was delayed. Dan, because beef cattle had been the lifeblood of Yellow Lance, turned always to the market page when he opened a newspaper. He knew that prime beef was bringing the best price in years, according to quotations at Kansas City and Chicago.

He emerged from the ridges and timber into the open heart of Springwater Basin. The view was so spectacular, he pulled up the horse and gazed. Timbered ridges rose to the west and north. He made out what seemed to be a line of fluted cliffs far to the south.

Springwater Basin was gorgeous. It was like a walled kingdom, guarded by its natural battlements and thick forests. To the north, distant, snow-tipped mountains peered over the rims, the source of a rushing river nearby.

Only the hand of man marred the vista. Less than two miles up the river a scatter of crude habitations stood in a dry flat, spread loosely on poor soil in a bend of the river.

A few rickety fences had been built of driftwood. A tiny

58

area had been cleared of scrub cedar and rabbit brush, and a pretense at gardens had been planted.

Dan had seen homesteaders attempt to dry-farm on the high plains along the Platte River, and break their hearts in agonizing battle against odds that were too great. But, in other places, he had seen them make the prairie bloom and prosperous towns spring up where there had been only loneliness.

He stared, pitying these people. Didn't they understand that the land they had preempted was so poor they'd never win? Even the brush that found lodgement was stunted, with roots that must cover wide areas in search of nourishment.

Springwater Basin was essentially stock country. Not a place for a man to bend over a hoe. This was a range for horsemen from which to look upward toward the mountains and the sky, to let the spirit soar.

The trail forked here. The wheel tracks that turned toward the patch of homesteads was new in comparison to the original road which swung eastward along the river. The old road was beaten by years of travel. This was the road Dan followed as he kneed his horse into motion.

After a mile, both the trail and the river veered directly southward. Mounting a rise, he saw the sprawl of a ranch spread ahead. Corrals, a windmill, barns and fenced fields where horses grazed. There were quarters for riders and for field hands.

A spur road to the ranch led beneath a huge cedar log, supported by stone pillars. From the log hung a heavy iron bell, burnished by time. Its rim bore a religious inscription in Spanish, molded when the bell had been cast.

Dan rode beneath the bell and neared the ranch. The main house of Spanish Bell was built of stone. Massive stone, carefully masoned so there was little room for mortar.

The doors and windows were Moorish in architecture. A carving of a Conquistador, which had seen the weather of many years, looked down from a niche in a small chapel which stood apart from the house.

Over the arched main portal was another inscription, carved in stone. *Casa del Rey*. House of the Kings. Royal House.

A stout Mexican woman in camisa and petticoat was

shaking out a rug as Dan rode across an echoing wooden bridge that spanned an irrigation ditch. She started to retreat toward the house, then paused gazing, as though to decide if he offered a threat.

Dan swung from the saddle onto a rock-built gallery that extended the length of the mansion. The gallery was lined with wrought-iron hitching posts, all of Mexican design and very old, but preserved by paint and attention.

Royal House had a wide, arched, brass-hinged door of heavy cedar. It was a ceremonial door and led, no doubt, to a big main room. Dan could imagine that colorful guests had entered those doors in the past.

A smaller door opened. Kathleen Royal appeared and moved out into the sunlight. She paused, waiting. "Please come in," she said. "Welcome to Royal House and Spanish Bell."

The thought came to him that, in keeping with the surroundings, she should be wearing a mantilla and a flowing Spanish gown, with a fan over which to gaze at him with eyes that were gray-green in this morning light.

Instead, she wore men's saddle jeans and boots, in defiance of convention. A spur jutted from the right heel.

A cowhorse, rigged for work in the brush, stood waiting. Its small saddle indicated it was for her use. Apparently, she had been about to head for the range, even though shadows under her eyes, and lines of fatigue still lingered as the aftermath of her long journey from Flag.

He tried to be disapproving of her garb, but the fact was that, on Kathleen Royal, anything would be feminine and shapely. As for convention, he surmised that here was a person who had caused tongues to wag many times.

Dan dismounted, and with studied deliberation, tethered the horse to a hitching post. Kathleen Royal stood at a distance, waiting for him to approach. Like a queen holding court.

Finally he walked toward her. "Good morning, ma'am."

"This is indeed a pleasure, Mr. Driscoll," she said.

"But not exactly a surprise, Miss Royal."

Her brows arched politely. "I love surprises. What can I do for you, Mr. Driscoll?"

"Maybe it's the other way around."

"I don't understand. You seem provoked about something, Mr. Driscoll. Have I offended you in any way?"

Dan drew the earring from his pocket and displayed it in the palm of his hand. "You left something behind when you pulled out of Flag the other night."

She uttered a controlled scream of delight. "My goodness! My Spanish Bell earring! I missed it that night. Where in the world did you find it?"

"In the last place I'd have thought of looking for it," he said.

"I was so worried," she said.

"I can imagine," Dan said. "Maybe you figured you'd never get it back. That would have ruined the set."

"How very nice of you to return it, Mr. Driscoll. I don't know how to thank you. My grandmother wore those earrings on her wedding day many years ago."

"You shouldn't chance losing them," Dan said. " 'Specially in the shirt pocket of a stranger. That's where I found it."

"Now, fancy that," she said lightly. "I never dreamed that was where it had gone. But I'd hardly call you a stranger, Mr. Driscoll. Not after the favor you did in preventing Alex Emmons from getting into trouble in Flag. I'm in debt to you doubly now."

She added, "Please come in. I'll have your horse cared for."

"I believe it's your horse," Dan said. "You—"

"—and I'm sure you could stand a nice, cold drink and a bite of food after your ride," she went on, as though not having heard him.

Dan's wrath suddenly subsided. He grinned. "I just can't say no." He meant to tell her she was wasting food and drink on him, but decided to let that wait until later.

"Bourbon or tequila in your drink?" she asked lightly, laying a hand on his arm and drawing him into the house.

"Neither," Dan said. "Something tells me I need to keep a clear head right now."

She took his hat and ushered him into a sitting room to the left of the big main room. "I'll only be a minute or two," she said. "Please sit down. There are cigars in that humidor."

Her spur clanked on the polished parqueted floor. She vanished down the hall. The room in which Dan waited was beamed, with deep-set windows, and furnished in a style of the past, but with taste and a sure eye for comfort.

When Kathleen Royal returned, she bore a tray on which sat two glasses and a cut glass pitcher in which ice tinkled in a clear liquid.

"Ice?" Dan exclaimed. "It can't be real!"

"You're lucky," she said. "It usually lasts until only mid-summer. The boys cut it on a lake in the mountains in winter and fill the icehouse. It will be gone in a few days, I'm afraid."

Dan sampled the contents of the glass she handed him. "Well," he commented. "It's different, at least. What is it?"

"Juice of the prickly pear apple," she said. "Mixed with other ingredients, according to my secret formula."

"You mean those thorny devils bear fruit big enough to produce nectar like this?"

"In this country they do," she said. "You're not from the southwest, I take it. Prickly pear is about the only fruit that seems to do well in Springwater Basin."

"Is that what those people I saw homesteading along the river are planting? Prickly pear?"

She gave him a slanting look. "I couldn't say. However, the Bible says that you reap what you sow."

"I've heard that somewhere else and not too long ago," Dan observed.

He finished the drink and placed the empty glass on the tray. "Thanks," he said. "I'll be shoving back to town now. That is, provided you'll loan me the horse for the return trip."

"I was hoping you had decided to hire out with our crew, after thinking it over," she said.

"Sorry," Dan said. "I doubt if some of the work you have here would be in my line."

"I'm sure you would be able to handle it. Perhaps it's the pay I mentioned that disappointed you. Forty a month might not interest you. I might raise the ante a trifle.".

"For instance . . . ?"

She caught her lower lip between her teeth for a moment, while she appraised him. "How much are you usually paid, Mr. Driscoll?" she asked.

"Depends on the job. And the hours."

"We're very short-handed. We should be shipping beef right now. Weeks ago, in fact."

"Meaning I'd have to earn whatever you offer?"

The tired anger that had been working inside her now flared to the surface. "Stop it!" she burst out.

Dan lifted his eyebrows, waiting with mock surprise.

"Stop being so bland!" she almost wept. "How much do you want?"

Before Dan could answer, she added, "Understand me clearly. I want no killing. Only protection for my father, myself, and my riders."

"You know who I really am, don't you?" Dan asked.

"Yes," she said listlessly.

"John Cass promised me he wouldn't—"

"Don't blame him. I was in Yellow Lance that night. The night Frank Buckman was killed. I had gone there to offer just what I'm offering you now. A job."

Dan stared. "I remember that they told me there was a woman waiting to talk to me," he said slowly. "You?"

"Yes. I was in the hotel sitting room among the crowd when you went out—you with your fancy guns and your swagger. You with your mustache and silk and diamonds. I had heard of Diamond Dan Briscoe. Who hasn't? I went to Yellow Lance to talk to you, to try to hire you. And your guns. John Cass is an old friend of my father's. I knew him when I was a child. I call him Uncle John, but he's not a blood relative."

"You made quite a long trip to hire fancy guns and a swagger," Dan said. "It actually isn't a cowhand you want, now is it?"

"I was wrong," she said. Her voice had the tremor of the strain and humiliation she was trying to hide. "I should have known better. I was desperate. But I know now you can't fight fire with fire without being burned."

"Defiled, you mean."

She became suddenly very composed, very cold and formal. "Thank you for returning the earring, Mr. Briscoe."

"Driscoll is the name," Dan said.

"If you wish it that way. I'll never mention your real identity if it would please you. You've had a long, hot ride. I really don't understand why. You could have left the earring with Ann Davis in Flag. Or even with Obie Willit in Flat Butte. He would have seen to it that I got it."

Dan lifted his hat. "Good day, ma'am."

"Exactly why *did* you come all this way to return it, Mr. —Mr. Driscoll?"

Dan looked directly at her. "I'm sure you know. I didn't really know myself until you came walking out of that door a few minutes ago."

She looked as though the breath had been driven from her. Color receded from her face, then came rushing back in a wild surge. She did not speak.

"What was your husband like?" Dan asked. "He could not have been a dull man. You're not the kind to waste yourself on a clod."

"Husband? I have had no husband."

"I must have misunderstood," Dan said. "John Cass said the Kate Royal he was talking about was a widow. I had the impression she was a middle-aged lady."

"Uncle John might have believed I was a widow," she said. "But not up in years, I'm sure. I was to have married a fine man. His name was Tom Randall. He was our range boss. He was killed a week before we were to have been married. That was nearly a year ago. Uncle John probably believed we had already been married."

"You say Tom Randall had been killed?"

"Goodby, Mr. Driscoll," she said abruptly. "You can leave the horse at the livery in town. The bill will be paid by Spanish Bell."

Dan turned to leave the house. As he reached the gallery, the creaking of wooden wheels sounded. A man had followed him from the door, manipulating a wheel chair in which he sat. A silk cloth covered his legs. He was a big man with weathered, sun-wrinkled skin, shaggy graying hair and a mustache to match.

"Who's this, Katey?" the man demanded.

Kathleen Royal spoke evenly. "This is my father, William Royal, Mr. Driscoll. I had lost one of Grandmother's wedding earrings in Flag, and Mr. Driscoll went to the trouble of returning it."

Bill Royal wheeled his chair close and extended a hand to Dan. His grip was powerful. "Excuse me for not gettin' up," he said. "Me an' my hawss fell into a coulee a while back, tryin' to turn a stampede at night. Me, I landed underneath. Left laig won't come around."

"I'm mighty sorry," Dan said.

"Thanks for fetchin' Katey's earring back," Bill Royal said. He studied Dan keenly. "You got the earmarks of a cowhand. You wouldn't be lookin' for—?"

"Mr. Driscoll is leaving," Kathleen Royal said quickly.

Bill Royal wanted to finish what he had been saying, but his daughter gave him a look. He went silent.

"Nice meeting you, Mr. Royal," Dan said. He walked to his horse, freed the reins and mounted. A horseman came across the irrigation bridge at that moment, his mount at a gallop.

The arrival was the tall, impulsive Alex Emmons. He was in the working garb of a cowhand. Brush-scarred chaps were buckled on his legs. Dust lay in creases on his shirt. He was unshaven and looked tired. His jaw was still swollen from the blow Dan had delivered, but he evidently had escaped any lasting damage.

He eyed Dan frowningly. "Who are you?" he demanded, halting his horse so as to block the path of Dan's mount.

Dan realized he was still a complete stranger to Alex Emmons. Evidently Kathleen Royal had not told Emmons exactly what had happened to him that night in Flag.

"I'm leaving," Dan said, and tried to move his horse ahead.

"Just a minute!" Emmons snapped. "Katey, who—?"

"It's all right, Alex," Kathleen Royal spoke sharply. "Mr. Driscoll went to considerable trouble to do me a favor. He's on his way back to town, if you'll get out of his path."

"Favor? What kind of a favor?"

"He returned a piece of jewelry I had lost," she said. "I apologize for Alex, Mr. Driscoll. He's doing what he thinks is best."

"I'm sure he is," Dan said.

"All right," Alex Emmons said angrily, and moved his horse aside. "But, after this, I do my own apologizin', Katey."

Dan looked back as he rode across the irrigation bridge. Emmons had dismounted and evidently was demanding information from Kathleen Royal.

Dan once more thought of handsome, impetuous Frank Buckman. He held great tolerance for Alex Emmons, even though the two of them had been flint and steel in that brief encounter. It was evident that Emmons was in love with Kathleen Royal and was quick to be jealous.

Dan rode heavy and listless. He had stood in the presence of great beauty and had turned his back on it. Its magic had burned him, leaving a scar. But all that Kathleen Royal had wanted of him was his reputation as a gunman.

The sun was blazing hot on his shoulders and he was grateful when his mount carried him into the shade of a stretch of scattered pines.

His horse suddenly halted, its ears pricked. Off the trail, another horse had appeared in the timber. The animal was caked with lather and dust. It bore a saddle that had slipped. It moved at a crabwise walk, for it had the weight of a man, dragging from a stirrup.

The animal halted, quivering as though thankful help had arrived at last, when Dan reached its side. The man's right foot was caught. He was bloody and moaning. He wore the chaps, leather cuffs and chin strap of a brush rider. His face was discolored and gashed. Not all of that damage had been caused by being dragged. Dan realized the man must have been brutally beaten with fists or perhaps boots.

The victim began moaning. "Don't hit me ag'in!" he croaked. "You'll kill me."

Dan removed the man's hat. He was bald-pated, with a fringe of graying hair. He must be pushing sixty, Dan decided. He freed the foot from the stirrup and carried him to the shade of a tree. The river was a hundred yards or so away. Dan ran to the stream and brought back water in his hat. He washed away some of the blood and dust.

The man's eyes opened. He looked up at Dan, terror returning. "You're all right now," Dan said soothingly. "What happened?"

The man could not answer. His horse bore the Spanish Bell brand. Dan decided this was the same rider he had sighted from the stage the previous day.

He brought more water. That revived the man so that he attempted to sit up, but failed.

"Easy, old-timer," Dan said. "You're from Spanish Bell, I take it. You lie here while I hustle to the ranch and have a wagon sent out for you while someone goes to fetch a doctor. Do you understand?"

The man mumbled incoherently. He gazed around, the terror still upon him. He apparently decided that only Dan was present and nodded that he understood.

Dan rode away. The pound of the horse's hoofs on the

bridge brought Kathleen Royal hurrying to the gallery, followed by her father in the wheel chair. Alex Emmons came from the corral, his saddle over his shoulder. Emmons dropped the saddle and came at a run.

"Man hurt!" Dan explained. "A mile or so down the road. Looks like he was beat up by someone, and then was dragged when he fainted and fell from the saddle. He was riding a Spanish Bell horse. Old-timer. Bald. About sixty, I'd say."

Alex Emmons smashed a fist savagely into his palm. "That'll be poor old Baldy. The dirty, filthy, yellow cowards. Picking on an old man."

"It's my fault!" Kathleen Royal sobbed. "Who'll be next? I never should have let Baldy go back to riding range again. Is he hurt very bad, Mr. Driscoll?"

"No telling," Dan said. "You'll need a wagon to carry him in. Somebody ought to ride for a doctor, if there's one in Flat Butte."

"I'll hook up the wagon," Alex Emmons said, and hurried away.

"Saddle my horse, Alex," Kathleen called. "I'll get the medical kit together."

A blocky-shouldered Mexican *vaquero* appeared, and began helping Emmons harness a team to a weathered stake wagon.

Dan rode to the corral. Alex Emmons pointed out a horse to be cut for Kathleen, and told him where to find her saddle. Dan had the mount rigged by the time she came running from the house, a leather pouch slung over her shoulder.

She and Dan rode ahead, with Emmons and the Mexican following in the wagon. They found the beaten man sitting where Dan had left him.

Kathleen fought back tears as she knelt beside him. "How did it happen, Baldy?" she choked as she began dabbing away blood and dust from his face.

Baldy had to try a time or two before he could form words. "It was them two roughs thet Livvy Shannon hired. Tom Smith an' Jim Martin. Somebody cut thet wire fence along the river, an' some o' our stock crossed over an' got onto the claims o' them squatters. There wasn't nothin' there to eat but rabbit brush anyway. I was roundin' 'em up when them two showed up. They said I'd cut the fence

67

an' shoved the cattle onto the boomers' land. They dragged me off'n my horse an' mauled me 'til I thought I was done fer. I managed to git back in the saddle after they'd gone. That's all I can recollect."

Dan and the *vaquero*, who said his name was Emilio Sandez, brought more water. Kathleen Royal doctored Baldy's injuries. He had deep cuts on his face and body. His assailants had put the boots to him, and the chances were he had a broken rib or two.

"Alex, head for town and fetch Doc Anderson," Kathleen said. "Baldy, you're going to be all right, but you'll need some expert stitching, and you may have a broken left wrist."

"I been sewed together before," Baldy croaked. "An' I lost count o' busted arms an' laigs years ago." His spunk was returning. "I been worked over by bad horses more'n once, but this is the first time I let human devils git away with it."

He eyed Kathleen accusingly. "If'n only I hadn't listened to you an' had packed Old Cedar with me, like I wanted, it'd have been a different story. From now on, I pack a gun when I ride range, an' I ain't lettin' no calico talk me out'n it."

Kathleen said nothing. Tears ran down her cheeks. Her hands shook as she and Emilio helped Baldy into the wagon. Alex Emmons mounted his horse and rode away toward Flat Butte.

Emilio handled the wagon and held the team to a walk as he headed for the ranch. Kathleen mounted, rode alongside the wagon and said something to Emilio in Spanish. Whatever it was, Emilio was startled.

"Where are you going, *querida mia?*" he spoke, protesting, and Dan knew that he framed the sentence mainly in English for his benefit.

"I'll be back soon," she said, returning to English also. "Josefa can take care of Baldy until the doctor comes."

"Please, please, señorita!" Emilio pleaded. "Come home weeth me! I do not like the look in your face. You weel get into very, very bad trouble if you—"

Kathleen had wheeled her horse, and was riding away.

Emilio appealed to Dan. "Stop her, señor! She has gone loco!"

Dan, too, had not liked the expression on Kathleen's

face. He had seen that same fixed glare in the eyes of men who were about to start on a rampage.

He swung his horse, and rode in pursuit.

CHAPTER SEVEN

Kathleen Royal's mount had built up a considerable lead. Dan decided against attempting to shorten the gap, for the time being. He was hoping she might relent and turn back.

She continued to push her horse. After half a mile, she left the road and took to the flats along the river. At first, Dan believed she was heading for the Shacktown the homesteaders had created. However, her horse forded the stream at a shallow stretch half a mile from the settlement, and passed through a break in a two-wire fence that skirted the south fringe of the river—the same break, no doubt, that had brought on Baldy's encounter with Shep Sand and Gid Marko.

Kathleen veered west, paralleling the river. This carried them abreast of Shacktown, and Dan could see two or three women and several children staring at them from among the habitations.

Even though he had not seen her look back, Dan was certain Kathleen knew he was following her. She was making a point of ignoring his pursuit in an attempt to prevail on him to abandon the attempt. Whatever purpose she had in mind, she evidently was determined to go through with it.

Dan continued to stay within reasonable distance. She had eased the pace in order to spare her horse, but there was no change in the dogged grimness with which she rode. Dan wondered if she was armed. There was no rifle on the saddle, and no pistol in sight, but that did not mean she could not have a short gun concealed.

She passed an opening in a barbed wire fence by way of a wooden cattle guard, which her horse picked its way carefully across. Dan's mount also negotiated the guard. A pair of wagon tracks came in off the flat to pass the fence by way of this opening, but no vehicle or rider had used this trail in a long time. The tracks made by Kathleen's mount were the only marks in a road made virgin by months of wind and weather.

Not far beyond the fence, they skirted the river again. Flat Butte rose massively to the right. They soon began mounting a steady ascent toward a rounded hogback which connected the big butte with a second, table-topped eminence that had been previously hidden from view by its larger neighbor.

Springwater River had cut its way through this ridge. Their route led them at times along the rim of the gorge. Dan glimpsed white water now and then and heard the roar of rapids that must have been two hundred feet below.

The hummocks and smaller ridges carried a pattern of narrow trails cut by small hoofs. They had been carved by animals that could find sustenance on almost perpendicular slants. Dan knew now that they had left Spanish Bell range when they had crossed the line fence. This was sheep country. Shannon country.

The elevation they reached commanded miles of the basin eastward. Looking back, he could see Royal House and its web of corrals and meadows, tiny at that distance, but sharply defined.

He followed the way across the rounded summit. An easy slope descended to a plateau, broken by draws and small gorges. Two miles or more ahead, on a wide flat, stood the buildings of a sheep ranch, shaded by cedar, with a windbreak of poplar along the channel of a ditch that brought water to a sizable pond.

Sheep pens, and long shearing and lambing sheds, all unused at this season, flanked the pond. Wool wagons stood with tongues elevated beneath shed roofs, along with three unused herder wagons with their typical round, sheet-iron tops from which stovepipes jutted.

The main house, like the home of Kathleen Royal, was built of stone, and apparently in the same pattern, by the same artisans. And dating back as many years.

Kathleen was riding directly toward the sheep ranch. Dan spurred his tiring horse and began closing the gap between them. There was activity at the ranch ahead. Men were saddling horses. Harness teams were being brought out and hooked to two of the wool wagons.

All this halted. Faces turned to stare as Kathleen Royal

came riding in. There were six men, and all were Basques by their garb, except one. The exception was the tall, sinewy man who had met Lavinia Shannon at the stage station. He wore a duck jacket, jeans bagged over cowboots and a round, undented hat. He also packed a holstered six-shooter. A rifle stood close at hand, evidently ready to be placed in the scabbard on the saddle of the horse the lean man had been about to mount.

Lavinia Shannon appeared from the main house. She wore a cotton house dress and had arranged her gray hair in a plaited bun at the back, and severely parted at the front. She looked old and gray and tired. And also unyielding.

Her grandson followed her. Lavinia Shannon shaded her eyes, peering at the approaching riders. She turned and spoke to the six-year-old boy. From the gesture she made, Dan knew she was ordering the lad back to the house. Chad Shannon did not obey.

Kathleen Royal did not slow the pace of her horse as she rode past the men. The tall one took a stride to intercept her, but she lifted the coiled quirt from the saddle horn and raised the loaded handle menacingly, driving him back.

She raced her horse toward Lavinia Shannon. The older woman, instead of retreating, moved on foot to meet the threat of the oncoming animal. She stood straight and challenging in the face of this danger.

Kathleen Royal dragged her mount to a halt only a few yards short of riding down the other woman. "Lavinia," she said between lips that were still ashen and taut, "if another of your hired ruffians ever again injures any of my crew, I'll hold you for it, personally."

The tall man came running to intervene. Dan arrived and yanked his horse into the man's path. "Stay out of this," he said.

The tall man had the same features, the same strength of character as Lavinia Shannon. His reaction was to go for his six-shooter. And he meant to fight.

"Wait, Heber!" Kathleen Royal shouted. "He's not armed. He's not in this."

Heber Shannon paused. He slowly slid his gun back into its holster.

Lavinia Shannon spoke. She had never taken her eyes

71

off Kathleen Royal. "The next time any of your people cross that line fence, they'll be shot. That includes you, Katey. We've buried enough dead. We've endured our last pile-up."

"I've also reached a limit, Lavinia," Kathleen said. "Baldy Strapp was beaten within an inch of his life today by those gunmen who pose as homesteaders. Baldy is up in years. I had pensioned him to an easy job for the rest of his life, but, because riders are afraid to hire out to Spanish Bell these days, Baldy went back to working cattle out of loyalty to me. After this, turn your wolves loose on someone who has a chance of defending himself."

"Speaking of wolves, there'll be plenty to fatten them for the next few days," Lavinia Shannon said. Her voice had the same metalic quality Dan had heard in Kathleen. "We were just starting out with the wagons to salvage what pelts we can. If the river smells of tallow and rotting mutton for the next few days as it flows past Spanish Bell, you'll know your night riders did their job well."

"What are you talking about, Lavinia?"

"As if you didn't know! Ride over to The Narrows. It's only a couple of miles. You might enjoy the sight of two hundred head of our lambs, mangled on the rocks, or floating dead in the river. They were driven over the edge of the bluff at daybreak by masked men. Two of our best dogs were killed. The herder escaped with his life only because he managed to get away into the brush. They were shooting at him."

"I know nothing about this," Kathleen said.

"Perhaps. Perhaps not. At least your father does. When you ride to The Narrows, take a look at the brand on a dead horse that's lying near where the sheep were driven over the bluff. I believe you'll recognize your own Spanish Bell brand. It's one of your quarterhorses that your father bred. We found it with a broken leg at daylight. My son shot it to end its misery. It had been ridden by one of the masked men who piled up the flock."

"That can't be true!" Kathleen exclaimed. She wheeled her horse and headed in the direction Lavinia Shannon had pointed. Dan joined her.

They rode in silence. The distance was less than two miles. Reaching the gorge where the river boiled more than a hundred feet below, they followed the rim for a distance. They pulled up and stared in silence.

The flock had plunged down a sheer drop. Dead animals were lodged in heaps against the base of the ledge. Carcasses floated in eddies in the river, or had been trapped by boulders in the center of the rapids. Many others, no doubt, had been swept away.

Kathleen gazed, fighting nausea. It was Dan who located the dead horse. He rode to it, and, without dismounting, gazed at its brand. Its saddle and bridle had been removed.

Kathleen did not approach. There was no need. She swung her horse around and headed back. Slowly now. The tears had ceased. She sat exhausted in the saddle, all the fire and spirit drained out of her.

She attempted to veer wide of the sheep ranch, but Lavinia Shannon and her son would have none of that. They climbed into one of the wool wagons, and drove to intercept them, the wagon lurching over the hummocks of grass.

"Well?" Lavinia Shannon demanded.

"I tell you again, Lavinia, I know nothing about this," Kathleen said. "Nor does my father, I promise."

"That's what you and your father said when our best rams were shot last winter. And when my husband died of exertion, trying to save a wool wagon when its brakes failed, and it and the team went through the ice in the river. Somebody had pulled the bolt out of the brake-rod. And there was the time that flock had been left to the wolves after our herder was terrorized into deserting by masked riders who—"

"I say it for the last time, Lavinia. Spanish Bell had nothing to do with any of those things."

"Have you asked your father? Just because Bill Royal is in a wheel chair doesn't mean he's completely harmless. He can still use his brain. He can tell his hired gunmen what to do and how to do it, so as to drive us to ruin."

"And who put him in a wheel chair, Lavinia?"

Lavinia straightened, but did not answer. "His horse didn't fall into that coulee accidentally after our beef holdout had been stampeded," Kathleen said. "It was shot. Where were your two hired homesteaders that night, Lavinia?"

Lavinia Shannon laughed mirthlessly. "It's an old way, Katey, blackening the kettle, then blaming someone else. Speaking of hiring riders, I suppose you know nothing about this man who's with you."

"Why should I?" Kathleen answered. "He's only a cowboy, looking for work. He's leaving Flat Butte. He's seen all he wants of this country, I imagine."

"Let's hope that's true," Heber Shannon said. "He don't stack up like a cowhand to me. I smell gunman."

Kathleen kneed her horse into motion, and the Shannons made no further move to stop her. Dan rode with her.

Heber Shannon shouted after them, "Tell your riders we shoot to kill from now on if they cross our fences. Night or day."

After they were at a distance, Kathleen began to weep. "I grew up with Heber and Abel Shannon," she sobbed. "We went to school together. Lavinia was like a second mother to me. Now, Abel is dead and Heber tells me he'll shoot to kill. What has happened? How did we come to such terrible hatred?"

Dan said nothing. Words were useless. Her grief ran too deep, the tragedy too poignant. He waited for the storm to ease. They left Shannon range, crossing the cattle guard at the fence before he spoke.

"Tell me about it," he said. "Don't keep it bottled up."

"What do you want to know?" she asked tiredly.

"You say your families were friends in the past. But, sheep and cattle don't mix, so I've been told."

"They don't usually fight each other, either," she said. "There have been sheep and cattle feuds, of course. But there has also been sheepmen against sheepmen, and cattlemen against cattlemen. It isn't a matter of cattle against sheep. It's humans against humans."

She added fiercely, "Greed against greed!"

"Is that what started it? Greed?"

"What else? The Shannons decided they wanted to spread out. The only direction they can spread is into Spanish Bell range."

"When did they first get that notion?"

She removed her hat, aimlessly trying to discipline her thick hair with her fingers while she thought back. "It's been building up for—it must be going on two years now.

74

It's been about a year since Abel Shannon and Tom Randall were killed."

"Abel Shannon was a brother of the one back there, I take it. How was he killed?"

"From ambush at night," she said. "The same way Tom was shot."

"Retaliation? An eye for an eye?"

She did not answer for a long time. "I don't want to talk about it," she finally said desperately.

"From what I gather, your families were friends for years, then got into a frame of mind to start drygulching each other. Something must have started it."

"We learned the Shannons weren't exactly the friends they pretended to be. We were told they intended to buy us out cheap, or break us so we'd have to sell. Matt Shannon accused my father of passing gossip about the Shannons that wasn't true. We heard the Shannons were trying to get their hands on a mortgage the bank in Flat Butte holds against Spanish Bell. One thing led to another. Then my fiancé was murdered."

"By the Shannons?"

"Probably not by them in person. More likely by some of those fake homesteaders they've brought in to steal our cattle and cut our fences."

"Such as the one who tried to crowd Emmons into a gunfight in Flag?"

"Yes. That awful Tom Smith, if that's his real name, which I doubt. And that other one who calls himself Jim Martin."

"Their real names are Shepley Sand and Gideon Marko," Dan said. "Killers. The pure quill. Very bad. Maybe you've heard of them."

"Yes! Oh, yes! Are you sure?"

"I'm sure."

"Do they know you?"

"I don't believe they do."

"Then how is it you know them?"

"By reputation, mainly. However, I've seen Shep Sand fight in the ring. I've read descriptions of Gid Marko, and it was known that he usually ran with Sand. You called all these homesteaders fakes. They can't all be like Sand and Marko. I saw women and children around those shacks."

"I suppose some are genuine. The majority of them, probably, although they're the kind who never really stay anywhere permanently. Someone posted advertisements in railroad stations as far east as Dodge City, saying there was free land to be had in Springwater Basin. That brought a rush. The real homesteaders moved on when they saw the kind of land it was. The others stayed. I doubt if many of them have wasted a homestead right by filing. They're living free, so why bother?"

"Free?"

"Someone is furnishing them with food and clothing. The women dress better than they ever did in their lives."

"Shannon money?"

"What else? Shacktown serves as a blind for bringing in men like the two you named to drive us to ruin."

"Ruin? Is it that bad?"

"We're in so deep at the bank Sidney Kain says he can't give us an extension. Obie Willit at the store is an old friend, but he can't carry us any longer either. He already holds two of our promissory notes, and wants to be paid."

"From talk I heard in Flag, the Shannons don't seem to be exactly rolling in money," Dan commented. "How can they afford to hire troubleshooters?"

"We didn't know what was going on until it was almost too late," she said. "We thought at first we were just having bad luck."

"Like that bunch of dead sheep in the gorge?"

Her lips tightened. "That *could* have been an accident. It wouldn't have been the first time a thing like that happened."

"That dead Spanish Bell horse? Was that an accident?"

"I don't know. I only know that it's now a case of survival. If we can hang on long enough, the Shannons will be the ones to go under."

"And then Spanish Bell will take over their range?"

She turned on him, her eyes blazing. "We don't want their range. We only want to be left alone. We're not grass hogs. Spanish Bell isn't a big ranch, and never will be as far as Dad and myself are concerned. All we ask is that we be allowed to make a living by selling beef, as we've done for years."

"That shouldn't be too hard to do," Dan said. "Prime beef on the hoof is selling at around forty-five dollars a head, the last time I looked."

"Not exactly on the hoof," she said. "At the stockyards in Kansas City. The trick is to get them there. We've got at least three hundred head of fat beef steers out in the brush —if we could only get them to the shipping pens in Flag."

"Why can't you?"

"In the first place, you can't swing much of a roundup in this rough country with only three riders, particularly when one of them is a woman."

"Why only three?"

"You're looking at one third of our crew. Alex and Emilio are the other two thirds. Baldy has been doing only odd jobs and taking care of irrigating the hay field. We usually carry five or six riders, and double that number at roundup or calf brand. But nobody wants to hire out to us, any more. Baldy isn't the first one of our men who has been beaten up by Tom Smith and his partner." She paused, then added:

"Three hundred head of beef at the prices today would be a fortune to us. Even a hundred head would see us through for a while, although I've seen the time when we were selling eight hundred to a thousand head a season. But rustlers have trimmed us down. Those squatters eat Spanish Bell beef. So do all our neighbors."

They rode in silence again and forded the river below Shacktown. When they reached the fork in the trail, she halted her horse and held out her hand. "Goodby, Dan Briscoe. I wish you the best of luck."

Dan did not accept her hand. He stirred his horse into motion, heading toward Royal House. "You win," he said.

She spurred to his side. "No! I can't let you do this!"

"Why not?"

"I tricked you into coming here."

"Yes, you did just that."

"I took advantage of you, because—well, because—"

"Because you're a woman. And a very attractive one."

She smiled wanly. "If so, it's all the more reason why you should never have come to Spanish Bell. After those two young men were killed that night in Yellow Lance, Uncle John Cass told me you had resigned as marshal. He said you were through with guns and violence. I didn't believe it. I only knew Diamond Dan Briscoe by reputation. I was sure money would talk. I hadn't been honest with Uncle John. I hadn't told him the truth about Springwater

Basin. I prevailed on him to urge you to at least take a look at it. I stayed with Uncle John and his wife until you left Yellow Lance. As a matter of fact, I was on the same train to Kansas City. I was right back of you in the line at the ticket window in the station there when you asked about the fare to Flag. I decided it would be better if I arrived in Flag a day later than you did."

"And now I'm here—in Springwater Basin," Dan said.

She looked at him levelly. "There's nothing for you here. Nothing but violence, and perhaps death."

Dan kept riding ahead. "Is there any one else?" he asked. "The memory of a dead man, maybe? Tom Randall? I can't fight that."

"No," she said. "But I won't let you—"

"Emmons and myself won't be able to cut out three hundred head and trail 'em to market, all at once," he said, "but we can do it a step at a time. Say, forty, fifty head at a crack. By snowtime, if we stick with it, we might have the herd trimmed down pretty well, and money in the bank."

He added, "There's one condition. I'm just a cowhand named Dan Driscoll. Nobody, and I mean nobody, is to know about Yellow Lance. Not even your father. Is that a deal?"

"I'm afraid Dad already knows," she said.

Dan was surprised. He was remembering the heartiness of Bill Royal's handshake. It had been sincere. Friendly.

"Anybody else?" he asked. "Emmons?"

"No," she said. She looked at him and her eyes were suddenly again bright with tears. But tears of a different kind. "It's been so long since anyone offered to help us," she said huskily. "You know I can't refuse. For my father's sake. And for mine."

Bill Royal sat in his blanket-padded chair on the gallery, crutches at his side, as they rode up and dismounted. Josefa came to the door and hovered in the background, listening. Alex Emmons walked from the bunkhouse and strode onto the gallery. He glared challengingly at Dan, obviously resenting his return, and stood at Bill Royal's side, waiting.

"How is Baldy?" Kathleen asked.

"He'll be all right," her father answered. "The doc patched him up, but he won't be riding for quite a spell.

Busted wrist an' some cracked ribs. They worked him over real good. We got him bedded down in the back bedroom."

"Dan Driscoll has decided to hire out with us," Kathleen said. She was trying to be matter-of-fact about it, but failed. She was taut, dreading her father's reaction.

Bill Royal's sun-faded eyes became unreadable under his thick brows. Dan believed there was deep regret in the rancher's mind. Also a bitter acceptance of the inevitable.

"You're travelin' mighty light, ain't you, Mister Driscoll?" he asked. He had put just the slightest emphasis on Dan's assumed name.

"My belongings are at Sim Ricker's hotel in town," Dan said. "I'll have to borrow a saddle until I can buy one."

"I didn't mean exactly that," Bill Royal said. "What you need is a—"

His daughter spoke hastily, "Mr. Driscoll will take Baldy's place. We'll have to market beef in small bunches that we can handle. It's the only way."

"It means ten times the work," her father said. "You an' Alex will be wore down to skeletons before fall. An' Mister Driscoll, too, if he sticks it out that long."

"I'll give it a try," Dan said.

"Come on, *Mister* Driscoll," Alex Emmons said curtly. He was taking his cue from Bill Royal, and was putting emphasis on the overly polite title. "I'll pick out a bunk for you to sleep in. You'll need it whenever the chance comes. Sleep—that is."

Dan followed Emmons to the bunkhouse. It was a comfortable structure, built in an L-shape, with a rock fireplace in the angle, cold and black at this season. The bunks were curtained for privacy. Beneath the mattresses were springs. Dan's brows lifted.

"Cowhands here get the best deal in Arizona," Emmons said. "Katey saw to it this place was made home-like."

"It's surprising they don't stay on," Dan commented.

Alex Emmons gave him a slanting look. "Ain't it?" he said dryly. "Take your pick of 'em. This one is mine. That one was Baldy's. Take any of the others that suits you."

"How long since they've been used?" Dan asked.

Again Alex eyed him. "We had almost a full crew up to about a year ago. Then they started drawin' their time an' pullin' out."

"That would have been about the time Tom Randall and Abel Shannon were killed, wouldn't it?" Dan asked.

"Just about, Mister Driscoll."

"Are folks around here in the habit of addressing cowhands as mister?"

"Not usually," Alex answered. "It's only the ones we ain't sure of that we're polite to."

"And you're not sure of me?"

"Why should I be? I don't know anything about you."

A hand knocked on the side of the building. Kathleen spoke from outside the door. "Are you decent? May I come in?"

She joined them. "I want to explain to you that I rode over to the Shannon ranch while you were going to town to fetch the doctor for Baldy," she said.

Alex nodded. "Your Dad told me. He watched you through field glasses until you crossed the ridge. *Mister* Driscoll, here, followed you."

"They've had another pile-up," she said. "They lost two hundred head. They say two masked men drove the flock over the rim at The Narrows last night."

Alex rolled a cigarette. There was a tough, twisted smile on his lips. "So?" he asked.

"The horse of one rider broke a leg and was abandoned, according to Lavinia Shannon. It was one of our animals. It was that blaze-face sorrel from your string, Alex."

Alex lighted his cigarette. "Blast the luck!" he said. "That was Jerry Whitestar. My best night horse."

"Who was with you, Alex?" she demanded. "Was it Baldy?"

"Are you saying I piled up them woolies, Katey?"

"I'm asking, not saying."

"I turned old Whitestar out to pasture a week ago," Alex said. "I'd been workin' him hard. Somebody must have helped themselves to him."

Kathleen was silent. Dan surmised she was wishing she could believe that. "The situation is wretched enough," she said. "If we start night riding like they do, there'll be only one end to it. More killings, until one side or the other is wiped out."

"I didn't pile up them sheep," Alex said stonily. "Maybe I wish I had. It's high time *somebody* started to hit back at Livvy an' Heber Shannon. But, I was asleep here all night in the bunkhouse. I wouldn't likely be hittin' the saddle ag'in after ridin' sixty miles with you from Flag, now would I? Baldy can tell you I was here in the bunkhouse."

"I don't want to ask Baldy," she said. "I'll take your word for it, Alex. If our side didn't do it, then who did?"

"Maybe we got friends we didn't know about," he said. He eyed Dan significantly.

"That's ridiculous," Kathleen said.

"Is it?" Alex blew smoke slowly from his lips. He continued to eye Dan. "When the boss asked you why you was travelin' light, he wasn't exactly meanin' you not havin' a warsack with you, *Mister* Driscoll. Seems like you don't pack a gun."

"I understand I'm hiring out to punch cows, not a trigger," Dan said.

"A man could get into big trouble out there in the slants if he didn't have a gun. His horse might pile him up an' bust his laig. He might get pinned down under a saddle. Rattler might fang him. Cow might horn him. Without a pistol, how would he let other folk know where he was?"

"I'll have to risk it," Dan said. "I get belly blisters, riding around with ten pounds of iron and leather hung on me. When do we start prodding some of these fat steers to market?"

"Tomorrow," Alex said. "Bright an' early."

"I take it we drive 'em to Flag to ship," Dan said. "Do we road brand for a trip like that?"

"No," Kathleen answered. "We only need inspection of brands before we ship at Flag."

"That'll help," Dan said.

"Provided we ever get them steers to Flag," Alex said. "It's a mighty rough trail."

"Meaning?" Dan asked.

"Didn't Katey mention that we started to Flag a month ago with more'n a hundred head? We still had a crew of five riders, not countin' Katey, who did as much work with the cattle as she did cookin'. We got to Flag with ten steers, an' just me an' Emilio an' Katey. The ten steers was so thin an' spooky from havin' been stampeded, we sold 'em to a wolf hunter for bait. Eight dollars a head. The rest were either dead in the coulees an' shinnery, or was hidin' deep in the mountains. We gathered another, smaller bunch two weeks ago. About thirty head. But—" He shrugged.

"Same thing?" Dan asked.

"That time they didn't shoot only into the cattle at night. We lost five good head of saddlestock. I had a slug through my hat. One of the three riders that had been scared into quittin' us on the other drive, had come back. But this time he rode off into the blue for keeps."

Alex added, "You still aim to earn that forty a month by not packin' a six-gun, *Mister* Driscoll?"

"You don't seem to believe that Driscoll is my right handle, Emmons," Dan said mildly.

"Now why would I think a thing like that?"

"What difference would it make?" Kathleen spoke quickly.

Dan had to find out if Alex knew his real identity. "Just why would I be wearing a blotted brand?" he asked.

"I wouldn't know," Alex said. "I haven't checked over the wanted posters in the postoffice in town lately."

Dan laughed. He was certain that Alex, although sure he was not what he pretended to be, did not know he was Diamond Dan Briscoe of Yellow Lance.

CHAPTER EIGHT

By nightfall the next day, they had only thirty-six steers in the holding corral at the ranch. Dan had learned during a day of heat and dust and aggravation that Spanish Bell beef might be fat, but it was also big and spooky. Previous stampedes had spread wariness through the brand.

He limped into the bunkhouse. He had been riding a borrowed saddle, which Kathleen had given him. It had been a long time since he had handled a throw rope. His hands were blistered, and chaps had rubbed the hide from his knees.

"Here's some liniment," Alex said, handing him a bottle. "Best cure-all in the world. It'll take care of them blisters in no time. Don't hold back on pourin' it on. The more the better."

Dan tested the "liniment" on one of the smaller blisters

on his hand. It burned like fire. It was the rankest type of tick dip. It would have meant a session of torture if he had followed Alex's advice.

He said nothing. He bathed in the irrigation ditch, used arnica on his blisters and aching muscles, and got into clean clothes. Kathleen called them to supper which was being served in the dining room in the main house.

Alex eyed him curiously when Dan came to the table, expecting trouble, but Dan made no comment and ate calmly. Bill Royal had nothing to say either. He sat at the head of the table in his wheel chair. Kathleen helped Josefa with the serving. She had ridden hard and recklessly during the day, doing as much of the work as the men.

"Don't you ever quit?" Dan said irritably. "What are you trying to prove? How tough you are?"

She did not answer. Emilio spoke. "It weel be much tougher tomorrow. Thees cattle, they are not as dumb as people say. They will all be holed up in the brush by daylight. They know we are starting a roundup."

Dan knew Alex was watching him, secretly puzzled by his calmness. Dan had brought the bottle of tick dip with him, hidden in a pocket, and it stood now beside his boot. He waited a moment when Alex was looking at Kathleen —which was a majority of the time—and poured a dollop of the concoction into Alex's coffee mug.

Alex lifted the mug. "I only wish I had a million dollars," he was telling Kathleen, "so you wouldn't have to worry your head about this sheep outfit."

He took a swig of the coffee. He exploded into a fit of sputtering and gasping. He ran from the room, heading for the kitchen to find water.

He finally returned, glaring at Dan. "Lucky I didn't swallow any o' that stuff," he said. "I might have been poisoned."

"Maybe next time I'll have better luck," Dan said.

But, he had made a mistake. He realized it now. He had humiliated the younger man in the presence of the one person in whose eyes Alex desperately wanted to appear mature and superior.

Alex finished the pie Josefa served, but kept his eyes on his plate. He left the table abruptly, with a mumbled excuse. Kathleen arose hurriedly and followed him out of the house into the warm darkness.

Bill Royal drew a sigh. "I was hopin' he'd git over it," he muttered. "But he ain't. Gettin' more mooney-eyed every day."

Dan said nothing. Kathleen's attempt to soothe Alex's injured pride was a mistake also. He doubted that Alex was aware her very real affection for him was not the kind he desperately wanted. Sisterly was the proper word. Dan knew how awful that could sound to a young man in love. He had had his ordeals of crushing agony and soaring hope a time or two at Alex's age.

He rolled a smoke. He was weary to the marrow, and wanted nothing more than to turn in, but he did not dare risk encountering Alex with Kathleen because of the mood Alex was in.

Bill Royal drew on his pipe for a time. Now he spoke. "Why did you change your mind about hirin' out with us, Driscoll?"

"Thanks," Dan said.

"Thanks for what?"

"For not calling me mister. That never sounds very friendly. And—" Dan was about to thank him also for not bringing up the fact that his real name was Briscoe. He decided to let Bill Royal choose the time and place for going into that matter.

Bill Royal smiled, and his gaze softened a trifle. "Katey's a mighty comely young lady," he said slowly. "She was to have been married to a fine man. She lost him."

Dan nodded. "She told me about Tom Randall."

"She might not get over a thing like that a second time. She's cut of fine stuff. She's like her mother, who left us years ago. I wouldn't want her to go through it ag'in."

When Dan said nothing, Bill Royal sighed again. "That's the reason you changed your mind, ain't it?" he spoke. "It's her, ain't it?"

"She told me there's nothing here for me," Dan said.

"Kathleen's a person of her word."

"I understand," Dan said. "I'd never do anything to hurt her."

"But you're stayin', even if there's nothing here for you?"

"I'm staying."

"Was it Alex that piled up them Shannon sheep last night?"

"He says not."

84

Bill Royal moved one of his legs, using both hands for the task. "If I could only ride!" he exploded. "I'd go over there an' have it out with 'em. Settle it, one way or another. This piece-meal fightin' ain't like the Shannons I used to know."

They heard Kathleen returning, and Dan arose as she entered the room. "I'll say good night," he said.

She walked with him to the gallery. "You shouldn't have done that to Alex," she said. "Ordinarily he'd have taken it as a joke. But he's changed."

"That's when you're around," Dan said.

"I don't care to go into—"

"Don't you know what you're doing?" Dan demanded.

She straightened. "What, exactly?"

"That night in Yellow Lance you saw a young chap get himself killed because he wanted to prove himself. A fellow in love is even more likely to go against odds too big to handle, but from which his pride won't let him back out."

"You're telling me I'll be to blame if Alex is killed, trying to prove that he's brave?"

"Has he ever drawn a gun in anger on a man?"

"Not to my knowledge."

"He's out of his depth here," Dan said.

"I've tried to send him away," she said shakily. "That is the truth. If you can get him to leave the Springwater I want you to do so."

"If I tried anything like that, it'd only put him more on the prod against me. It seems that we both are here for the same reason. You're that reason."

"No, no!" she breathed protestingly. She turned abruptly, and almost ran into the house.

Dan walked to the bunkhouse. He found Alex pushing shells into the magazine of a rifle. Alex had his black-holstered six-shooter buckled at his side. His bedroll and tarp lay on his bunk.

Dan eyed him. "Going somewhere?"

"I'm campin' out tonight," Alex said. "Down near the corral where I can keep an eye on the steers. In case we have visitors I aim to act as reception committee."

"A committee of two would be better," Dan said. "Can you fix me up with some sleeping gear?"

"What would you do," Alex asked caustically, "throw rocks at 'em?"

85

Dan hesitated, frowning. "All right," he finally said. "If there's a spare gun around, I'll pack it."

"Ever use a six?"

"I know which end the smoke comes out of," Dan said.

"I just bet a cookie you do," Alex said grimly. He pulled a locker from beneath his bunk, opened it, and handed Dan a .44. "I'll find a rag to wipe off the grease," he said. "I'll dig up a belt and holster. Also a rifle. The boss has plenty of artillery at the house. You can borrow Baldy's tarp an' soogans for tonight."

Emilio joined them, and the three of them bedded down at various points around the small corral where the cattle were held. But no visitors came out of the starlight to disturb their uneasy rest.

They were in the saddle before sunup the next morning. Kathleen rode with them. By noon of the second day they had sixty-five head of prime steers in the gather. The herd was too big for the corral, and they drifted it to the fenced horse pasture a mile west of the ranchhouse.

"That'll be all we can handle," Alex said. "We'll throw 'em on the trail in the mornin'."

"It *does* seem like a pretty small bunch," Dan said.

"We might have even more'n we can handle, *Mister* Driscoll," Alex said. "It's ninety miles to Flag. Rough country, an' rough people along the way. If these steers are spooked into the shinnery they'll head back to where we caught 'em, an' they'll be twice as hard to round up the next time. That's what happened before."

Dan's belongings were still in the hotel in Flat Butte. "I could stand a change of clothes," he said. "And a couple of new shirts. This one I borrowed from Baldy's wardrobe is two sizes snug. I want to pick up my own warbag. I'll be back by dark."

He saddled a fresh horse and headed for Flat Butte. Alex shouted something as he rode away. It sounded like a warning, but he pretended not to hear, and did not turn back. He had left the borrowed pistol at the camp, and he guessed Alex was trying to remind him of this oversight.

Reaching the fork in the road, he slowed his horse. He had become increasingly curious about Shacktown. Here was his chance for a closer look. It would take him only a mile or two out of his way.

He headed up the river. As he rode closer, he saw that

the majority of the habitations were merely rude hovels. Some consisted of wagon tarps spread on poles over depressions that had been shoveled in the earth. Others were formed of tarpaper or rusty sheet iron held by rickety frames of scrap lumber.

Only two structures had even a semblance of permanency. Even these could not be called homey. One was a stark, two-story clapboard affair. It apparently consisted of only an upper and a lower room, to which was attached a lean-to kitchen at the rear. The second building, one-story, with a flat-roof, and constructed of rough planks, stood about a hundred feet from the rear of the larger structure. Over its door was painted the word STORE.

The impression grew within him that none of this was genuine. At the first shack he passed, a young woman, frowsy-haired, but dressed amazingly in a cheap, but gaudy blouse and skirt, and high-heeled slippers, sat idly in a varnished rocking chair on the bare ground in the shade of the structure. A girl of about five, in soiled calico, joined the woman in staring with gawkish curiosity as he rode past.

Dan touched his hat. "Howdy, ma'am. Hello there, young lady. Pretty hot this afternoon, I'd say."

They did not answer. They merely stared. The aroma of beef being cooked, came from the hovel.

The few other inhabitants of Shacktown that he glimpsed also seemed to be able to dress much better than the appearance of their dwellings indicated.

He neared the two frame structures. The gabled, two-story building had dark window blinds, closely drawn. The effect was that of vacant eye sockets.

Two men emerged from this house. Shep Sand and Gideon Marko. Sand was in shirt sleeves, but Marko wore his black sack suit despite the midday heat. Marko had a tin cup in his left hand. The wind brought the odor of whiskey. Both men were carrying six-shooters in holsters.

Dan nodded, "Howdy."

Shep Sand measured him with cheerless eyes, his gaze resting for a space on the Spanish Bell brand on the horse. "What do you want?" he demanded.

"Just passin' through," Dan said. "Headin' for town."

"You're on the wrong fork, mister. You'll only get deeper into the hills in this direction. Nobody might ever find you if you dropped out of sight there."

"Now, I sure don't want to go where I'd never be heard of ag'in," Dan said. "I'm mighty obliged to you for the warnin', mister. My name's Driscoll. An' you?"

"That's the way back," Sand snapped, pointing down the trail.

Dan had seen all he wanted to see. He turned his horse and headed back. But, none of his questions had been answered. Instead, new puzzles had appeared. Shacktown was a jigsaw with many pieces missing. Even the two or three mongrel dogs that came to bark at his horse did so only half-heartedly, and more in good humor than opposition. Contrary to their usual lot in such surroundings, they seemed fat and well-fed.

One retreated to his bed in the shade, flopped down and began gnawing on a bone. A sheep bone. The dog's bed was a sheep pelt. Dan glimpsed the hide of a steer stretched on pegs for curing. The brand and earmarks had been cut out. A plump woman came to the door wearing a dress that was shapelessly made, but was obviously of new calico.

The frowsy-haired, young woman in taffeta and high heels still sat in her rocking chair as Dan returned. The small girl was running through the brush in pursuit of a butterfly. She had eyes only for her quarry, and the chase was carrying her toward the river. There were bogholes and mud sinks along the stream that were anathema to cattle and to ranch hands.

The child suddenly vanished in the brush. And did not reappear. Dan sent his horse galloping in that direction. The mother leaped to her feet and screamed, "Bessie!"

The child had tumbled down a four-foot cutbank into a treacherous bog of mud and water. She was struggling to grasp a handhold on the clay bank, but was only creating small landslides that forced her deeper. She was down to her waist, her strength almost spent.

Dan left the saddle, paying out his tied-down lariat. The horse, trained to meeting the strain of the rope, braced itself. He clung to the rope with one hand, lowered himself a stride down the cutbank, reached down, seized the child by an arm, and lifted her to safety.

"You're all right now, honey," he said.

The mother arrived. She was hysterical. "Bessie might have drowned," she sobbed.

"I doubt that," Dan said. "But she did get the scare of a lifetime, I'm afraid."

The mother calmed a trifle. "You're all muddy, mister," she said. "Look at what you caused, Bessie."

The child quit blubbering, and began to giggle. "He's a funny man," she said.

"You ought to see me without mud," Dan said. "You'd never quit laughing. Ma'am, if you've got a washtub, I'd appreciate a chance to sluice off my shirt front. It'll dry in a hurry in this weather. There's no real damage done."

He lifted the child on the horse. The woman, who said her name was Mrs. Hallie Barnes, racked along in her high heels to the shack, where he began removing the mud as best he could.

"Your husband is out working on your claim, I take it?" he remarked.

She uttered a sniff. "More likely he's in Flat Butte, hangin' around a saloon."

A blanket served as a door for the shack, but it was held back. Dan had a view of the interior, which was in disorder, but that was mainly because of abundance, rather than neglect. Cheap, new, varnished furniture took up the majority of the space. A gaudy table cover with gold tassels was almost buried in stacks of canned food and other staples that were piled on the table and beneath it.

Dan saw that Hallie Barnes was watching him. "Where are you folks from?" he asked.

She shrugged indifferently. "Here an' there. We been in Kansas an' Colorado. We was headin' for California when we heerd there was free land to be had down here."

She glared around, uttering another sniff. "Free land! No wonder it's free. Nobody but fools like my man would listen to such soft soap."

"It doesn't look like you're starving," Dan observed. "I smell beef cooking. Nor going without clothes to wear."

She bridled. "I reckon a body's got a right to decent grub an' clothes if it's offered."

"Offered?"

She subsided abruptly. She peered at his horse. "You're a cowboy from that ranch down the river, ain't you?"

"I hired out there today," Dan said.

"Today?" She studied him uneasily, torn between gratitude for helping the child, and some inner caution. He believed the fact he was unarmed allayed whatever fears she entertained.

"Why stay here, if there's no future?" he asked.

"Well, there just might be something to all this talk about irrigation an' buildin' a dam," she said. "Anyway, as long as Tom Smith an' his partner an' the bank want to pay us free board, we'd be fools not to stay. We kin move on to California any time."

"Tom Smith? What's he got to do with it?"

Caution won out with Hallie Barnes. "He runs the store here," she said. "Now, I thank you, mister, for savin' my—"

Dan refused to let her end the conversation. "Irrigation? Say, maybe I better stake out a claim myself. I've never used my homestead right."

"Maybe," she said dubiously. "To tell the truth, we ain't filed either. My man don't want to use his right 'til he's sure it won't be wasted. Ain't many of the others that have filed either. Both, I reckon you could get free grub, too, if you wanted to hang around a while."

"How do I go about that?"

"I really ain't supposed to talk about it," she said, "but everybody in Shacktown knows it. All you have to do is go talk to Mr. Kain at the bank in town. He'll fix things for you."

"Fix things?"

"He'll show you where to stake your quarter, an' he'll give you grub an' clothes to git along. A little money too."

"Why would he do that?"

"He calls it an investment. Says settlers will flood the country when the word gets around, an' everybody will git rich, includin' the bank."

Her voice had suddenly trailed off. Her face had lost color.

Dan turned. Shep Sand was standing a few yards away. He had approached quietly from the opposite side of the shack, and had probably been listening before stepping into view.

Sand spoke. "What was it you said your name was, mister?"

"You can call me Driscoll," Dan said.

"I reckon that's as good a handle as any," Sand said. "You came down from Flag on the same stage I was riding a few days ago, as I recollect. And now you're workin' for Spanish Bell?"

"I took a job there," Dan said. "But I might change to homesteadin'."

"Yeah? Why?"

"Sounds like it might be a better deal," Dan said. He walked past Sand and mounted his horse. As he rode away, he heard the woman chattering an explanation of the child's rescue. She sounded as though she was in mortal fear.

CHAPTER NINE

It was late afternoon when Dan unsaddled at the livery, and saw to it his horse was watered and fed. Despite the hour, the bank was still open. He crossed the street. The names of the bank's officers were lettered in gilt on the door. Obie Willit was listed as president and Sidney Kain as cashier.

There was only a single window in the iron grill, back of which stood an open roll-top desk and a big steel safe which was bolted to rings in the floor.

A thin-necked man in a stiff collar and dust jacket was playing solitaire at the desk. He looked up indifferently, and said, "What can I do for you?"

"I hear there's land for filin' down in the basin," Dan said. "I was told that a Mr. Kain at the bank could give me information about stakin' a claim."

The man came to his feet, the indolence gone. "I'm Sidney Kain," he said. "Who told you to see me?"

"I happened to talk to a feller named Tom Smith," Dan said. "I was told there might be money to be made in the basin if'n a man got in on the ground floor."

Sidney Kain studied him for a moment. "Why, certainly," the man said. "I'll see what I can do. Your name, please."

He scribbled the name Dan gave him, and looked at the clock. "Why, it's past closing time," he said. "I'll attend to this in the morning. See me then."

Dan nodded. He walked to the hotel, got his belongings and carried them to the livery. He left them there, telling the hostler he would be back shortly. He strolled to Mack's Place. The saloon was small and dingy, with a bar made of two thick cedar planks at the right, a pair of poker tables along the left wall, and a shabby pool table at the rear. He ordered beer. Mack, a fleshy man with a longhorn black mustache, drew the beer from a spigot into a glass mug.

Through the dust-fogged front window Dan had a view of the bank half a block down the street and on the opposite side. In fact, it had not been out of his sight for more than a few seconds at a time since he had talked to Sidney Kain.

The door of the bank was closed, and the curtains had been drawn. Sidney Kain now appeared on the sidewalk, evidently having emerged from a rear door. He wore a dark sack coat and a rusty derby hat.

Kain was peering around. Dan believed he was the person the man was trying to locate. As Kain approached the vicinity of Mack's Place, Dan dropped a dime on the floor, and bent out of sight of the window, pretending to search for the coin until Kain had proceeded past.

Straightening, he watched Kain enter Obediah Willit's Great Southwestern Mercantile. He left his beer unfinished and walked down the street. Passing the mercantile, he glanced in. Obie Willit kept his windows much cleaner than did Mack. Dan had a full view of the sizable store. A woman clerk was displaying a bolt of gingam to a feminine customer. A male clerk was waiting on a woman who had a market basket on her arm.

Obie Willit was closing the door of a cubbyhole office at the rear, and Dan glimpsed Sidney Kain seating himself in the visitor's chair at Obie's desk.

Dan returned to Mack's Place, ordered another glass of beer and waited. A quarter of an hour passed before Sidney Kain emerged from the mercantile. He was moving fast, with the air of a man with something very important on his mind.

Kain headed directly for Mack's Place, and came hurrying in. "Mack!" he exclaimed. "Do you know who that fellow really is who Katey Royal hired—!"

He became aware that Dan was standing at the bar. He stood petrified, his voice choking off in a gulp. Then he backed out of the saloon and hurried down the street.

Mack went to the window and stared in amazement. "You'd have thought Sid Kain had seen the devil!" he said.

"Maybe you guessed it," Dan said.

He left Mack gaping and walked out of the saloon. Sidney Kain, looking over his shoulder, was ducking into Sim Ricker's hotel. Dan moved down the street to the mercantile and entered.

Obediah Willit must have been at a peephole, for he emerged from his office like a jack-in-the-box. He came hurrying down the length of the room. "Well, well!" he boomed. "It's Dan Driscoll, ain't, it, if I recollect the name right? What can I do for you, friend?"

"I'm thinkin' of stakin' out a claim for myself down on the river," Dan said. "I want to know if you'll carry me for food an' possibles for a few weeks." He was deliberately making a mockery of his newly assumed role as an uneducated man.

Obie Willit studied him for a moment with unreadable eyes. "You ever done any sod-bustin', brother?" he asked.

"Nope," Dan said. "But I'm handy at other things." He let an eyelid droop slightly in a wink.

"How do you aim to pay?" Willit asked. "It'll be quite a spell before you can market a crop."

"I'm ridin' for Spanish Bell," Dan said. "I'll do my provin' up on the claim on the side. They pay pretty well out there for the right kind o' work."

"I might carry you on the books for a while," Willit said. "Anybody who works for Bill an' Kate Royal is welcome here."

Dan bought a supply of tobacco, two shirts and a few other necessities. When Willit added up the bill, he laid a goldpiece on the counter.

Willit's brows lifted. "You was askin' for credit," he said.

"As long as I got dinero there's no use goin' into debt," Dan said.

"Nor to an early grave," Willit said, sounding his booming laugh.

"Now, that's somethin' I really aim to avoid," Dan said.

He picked up his purchases. "If I decide to homestead, I'll let you know."

Willit nodded and stood watching him walk out of the store. Dan was hungry, but the supper bell at the hotel would not sound for an hour. However, the fragrance of chili and tamales drifted from El Cantina, which served food as well as liquid refreshments. He headed in that direction.

Passing the hotel, he glanced through the window. Three persons, including Sim Ricker, were peering into the street. They all suddenly pretended to be interested in something elsewhere, but he had been the object of their stares until he had glanced in their direction.

The head of the hosteler was jutting from the door of the livery office. It popped out of sight like a prairie dog darting to cover. A man in the rough garb and hide boots of a mule skinner emerged from the blacksmith shop. He halted uncertainly when he saw Dan, as though unable to decide what to do. He finally retreated hurriedly into the shop.

Dan entered El Cantina. The barkeeper, who evidently was also the owner, was long and lean, with weathered features that had taken punishment in the past. He moved stiffly on rheumy joints—the mark of a retired broncho buster.

"Beer, tamales, and chili, with plenty of tortillas," Dan said.

"I got no beer," the tall man said. "I got no tamales. No tortillas, no chili."

Dan looked at the beer spigot, which showed the drip of very recent use. Food simmered on a big stove at the rear, with a Mexican cook in charge. A man, who was the only other patron, finished off a mug of beer at the bar and hastily left the place.

Dan placed his hands flat on the bar and looked at the owner. "I might not take this kindly," he said. "Why isn't my money good?"

"I don't want none o' Bill Royal's cash," the bar owner said.

"I'll tell him that the next time I see him," Dan said.

"I reckon you'll see him soon. I hear he pays good money to the right kind of help."

"News gets around, doesn't it?" Dan commented.

"Bad news generally does."

"And just to think," Dan said mildly, "an hour ago, no-

94

body in Flat Butte was giving me a second look. Now, I'm the biggest tiger in the circus. The man-eater."

"You'll find the Shannons mighty tough to digest," the thin man said.

"You look like you rode your share of salty horses," Dan said. "Now you back sheep. And don't care much for Bill Royal. Any particular reason?"

"I don't cotton much to any man what imports killers, an' tries to bust a hard-workin' outfit like the Shannons, mister. I was borned on a cow ranch. I like cattle. I never walked sheep in my life, but that ain't the point. Bill Royal used to be a square dealer. He changed. I didn't."

"Who says Bill Royal has done the things you tell me?"

"It's as plain as the gun you ain't wearin' today," the man said. "Next time, you better pack iron. You an' them other two leppies that Bill Royal has planted among them homesteaders on the river. Now there's three of you ag'in the Shannons."

"You might have made out at taking the rough off bad horses," Dan commented, "but I'll bet you never was worth a hoot at reading brands."

He left El Cantina. More eyes were staring, more furtive faces, ashine with curiosity, popped in and out of doors.

He got his horse at the livery. The hostler was fawningly respectful. Crawlingly anxious to please.

"I take it," Dan said, "that you're for Bill Royal."

The hostler made sure they weren't being overheard. "I sure am," he whispered. "He always treated me square."

"And if you'd been told I had hired out to the Shannons, you'd be for the Shannons, wouldn't you?" Dan said. "You must get bow-legged, trying to walk both sides of the street at the same time."

He lashed his belongings on the horse and rode out of the livery. Flat Butte's main street had a deserted look. It was sundown. He saw the same furtive fade of eyes and faces into the shadows of doors and windows.

"The show's over!" he said aloud, savagely.

He rode back to Spanish Bell. He pushed the horse, driven by a bitter anger that would not burn out. And by a sort of despair.

Lamplight glowed in the windows of Royal House as he rode up. Josefa came to the door as he dismounted at the

95

gallery. "The señorita and the *patron* are waiting, señor. We have held supper for you. Emilio and the Señor Alex are with the cattle, standing guard."

Dan entered the dining room. Bill Royal laid aside a newspaper he had been reading. Kathleen came from the kitchen, bearing a steaming tureen.

Dan spoke. "You Royals have got your money's worth already. Flat Butte was ready to go up a tree today if I'd bared my teeth at them."

Kathleen carefully placed the tureen on the table and smoothed the ruffled, small apron she wore. She said nothing, waiting. Her father sat straighter in his wheel chair.

"You've played me for a fish on your line, haven't you?" Dan said.

Kathleen spoke exhaustedly. "Go on. Tell us why you say that."

"When did you send word to Obediah Willit that I was Diamond Dan Briscoe from Yellow Lance?"

Her head lifted. "Obie Willit? He knows? Him?"

Dan gazed at her for a space. He finally drew a deep breath. "I turned into a man-eater this afternoon in Flat Butte," he said. "Right before their eyes. Right before my own eyes. A killer. A man to be avoided."

He added, "I thought you had broken your word. I see I was mistaken."

She kept looking at him without speaking.

"Somebody there knew," Dan said. "He waited until now to let out the secret. Sidney Kain was told to spread the news. You should have seen those people when they realized they were looking at Diamond Dan Briscoe. They were afraid. Horrified. They were wondering who would be the first the monster would eat."

"I'm sorry," she said. "So sorry."

"Obie Willit must have recognized me right at the start as the killer from Yellow Lance," Dan said.

"Don't use that word."

"Killer? That's what you wanted when you went to Yellow Lance, wasn't it. A killer?"

"Please, please!"

"You played with pitch and now you're defiled. You want to repent, but it's too late."

96

"You're right," she said huskily. "And I am repenting. I was wrong in tricking you into coming here. But I am not defiled."

Her father spoke harshly. "Stop torturing her, Briscoe. It was my idea. I sent her to Yellow Lance to hire you. I couldn't go myself."

He added, his voice gentling, "It was all a mistake, Briscoe. I misjudged you, knowin' you only by reputation. Most of all, I misjudged myself. Even if you had been the kind I first figured—a killer—there'd have been no place for you at Spanish Bell. I came to my senses after I'd sent Katey to Yellow Lance. Goodby, Briscoe. This ain't your fight. I'm sorry. Sorry for everything."

Dan stood there for long seconds, looking at Kathleen. She was the one he had been searching for through the lonely years of his life. He had found her. And lost her.

"Goodby," he said, and turned to leave the house.

"Just a minute," Bill Royal said. "We've got something that belongs to you."

He rolled his wheel chair toward a carved highboy. Kathleen rushed into his path, halting him. "No!" she said fiercely. "He's finished with all that. Let him live in peace."

Bill Royal sat with a black frown for a space, then whirled his chair and left the room. Dan walked out of the room and out of the house. He mounted his horse. Kathleen came to the gallery and stood in silence for a moment.

"Some day this will be all over—one way or another," she said. Dan knew what she meant. It was a hope that he would come back to her—after the feud had ended, after the killings were finished.

Dan did not speak. He could not. He knew there would be no returning. Nothing could ever be the same again. In his heart he was saying, in misery, "My God! My God!"

He kneed the horse into motion. A gunshot sounded, faint in the distance. That touched off a muted drumfire of shots. Then came the deep, thudding roar of running cattle.

"The herd!" Kathleen screamed. "Alex! Emilio!"

Dan whirled his horse and raced through the ranchyard toward the meadow where the holdout of steers had been placed. He could still hear the cattle running. They were scattering in the darkness, heading for open range. Evidently they had torn through the smooth wire fence that enclosed the horse pasture. Two days of riding to round them up was lost. And these steers would be more wary, more difficult to bring in a second time.

"Alex Emmons!" Dan shouted. "Emilio! Don't shoot! It's Driscoll! Sound out! Where are you?"

Presently an answer came. "This way, *Mister* Driscoll." Even at a moment like this, young Emmons was hostile.

Dan located him in the starlight. Alex was mounted and had his rifle slung on his arm.

"You all right?" Dan asked.

"I wasn't hit by a bullet, if that's what you mean," Alex said. "Emilio's all right, too. He's out there somewhere. They wasn't shootin' at us. They shot into the cattle. They got a few steers. I saw a couple of animals down. The rest are gone."

"How many men jumped you?"

"I saw the flashes of two guns," Alex said. He added, "Just where were you at the time, *Mister* Driscoll?"

"The name," Dan said, "is Briscoe. Not Driscoll. Diamond Dan Briscoe. Maybe you've heard of him?"

There was a long silence. Emilio came riding up to join them. "You know something?" Alex finally spoke. "I had you tabbed, right from the start. You didn't look or act like a common cow pusher. Let's take a peek at your rifle."

"I don't happen to have one," Dan said.

"You could have cached it somewhere."

"Meaning that I'm playing both sides against the middle?"

"Isn't that the way your kind work? Money's money, no matter where it comes from."

A horse was approaching at a gallop. Kathleen's voice called out, and Alex shouted a response. She joined them.

"Thank heaven you and Emilio aren't hurt!" she breathed.

"They were picking off cattle this time," Alex said.

"Did you see them?"

"Only the flashes of the guns. I think there was only two of 'em."

Dan spoke. "Emmons seems to think I might have been one of them."

98

"No, Alex," Kathleen said. "Mr. Driscoll was at the house when we heard the shooting."

"Glad to hear it," Alex said. "By the way, he just told me his name ain't Driscoll. It's—"

"Briscoe," she said, "I've known that for some time. I'm responsible for his being here."

"Responsible? What do you mean, Katey?"

"I tried to hire him as a gunman."

"*Tried* to hire him? You mean he turned you down?"

"Emmons wonders if I might not be taking money from both sides," Dan said.

"No, Alex," Kathleen said. "I can tell you that is not so."

"How can you tell that?" Alex snapped. "What do you know about men like him? About killers?"

"I saw his face one evening in Yellow Lance after two men had been killed in a gunfight," she said. "I didn't believe what I saw. At least I forced myself to try to believe that. I tricked him into coming to Springwater Basin. I was wrong. He's through with all that. The guns, the kil—"

Again came the far, thin sound of a rifleshot. Then silence for a time. Dan rose in the stirrups. He believed he was hearing the faint sound of a woman screaming.

"The ranch!" Kathleen cried. "Josefa!"

They rode frenziedly to Royal House. The screaming of Josefa came nearer, forlorn and grieving.

Dan pushed Kathleen back when they leaped from their horses. He was first to enter the house. Josefa was on her knees, praying.

Bill Royal's body was slumped over the arm of his wheel chair. The chair was tipped crazily against the highboy in the living room. His fingers grasped the handle of one of the drawers in the cabinet as though he had been desperately trying to open it when death had defeated him. He had been shot in the back of the head.

CHAPTER TEN

Dan motioned to Alex Emmons to keep Kathleen back. He made sure it was futile to hope a spark of life might remain in Bill Royal. He lifted a fine lace cloth from a table and covered the rancher's body.

"It's no use," he said to Kathleen.

He lifted Josefa to her feet. "Did you see who did it?" he asked.

"No, señor," the woman sobbed. "I was in the kitchen. I heard voices. Very angry voices. I heard the *patron's* wheel chair moving, fast. Then the shot. And a horse galloping away."

"A horse? There was only one?"

"I am sure it was but one horse I heard."

Alex spoke harshly. "They spooked the cattle to draw us away from the house. Then one of them sneaked in."

"Is there a law officer in Flat Butte?" Dan asked.

"What do we want with the law?" Alex spat. "This is Bill Royal they murdered. We know who did it. One of those two leppies who pretend to be squatters in Shacktown. And we know who ordered it done."

"The law must be notified," Dan said. "And the coroner."

"Dr. Anderson acts as coroner," Kathleen said. She stood beside her father's body, a hand stroking the cloth that covered him. Her skin was waxen, her voice dull. "There's no law officer in town. We'll telegraph the sheriff at Flag. He will come down."

"That'll take days," Alex raged. "And all he'll do is nothing, like when Tom was murdered."

"What about the other side?" Dan asked. "I understand one of the Shannons was killed also a time back. What did the law do about that?"

Emmons shrugged. "Ben Hughes doesn't want any part of what goes on down here."

"Anyway, he should be notified," Dan said. "And the doctor should be sent out here. This must be handled ac-

100

cording to law. An inquest should be held, and a death certificate signed. You better head for town."

"Emilio can take care of it," Alex said.

"And you?"

"I've got other plans."

"Such as maybe riding to Shacktown with a gun in your hand to take on Shep Sand and Gid Marko."

Alex stared at him. "Who? You don't mean that's who them two really are!"

"You seem to have heard of 'em."

"Yeah, I've heard of that pair. The Shannons will have to shear a lot of sheep to pay the kind of money those two draw for killing people."

Alex turned and strode out of the house. "Stop him!" Kathleen exclaimed. "Please! You did it before."

"This is getting to be a habit," Dan said. He looked at Emilio. "Get your throw rope," he said.

Alex was in the act of mounting when Dan reached his side. "Let's talk this over," Dan said, placing a hand on his knee.

"This is one time I don't let anyone stop me," Alex said. "Stay out of this, Briscoe. This is for Bill Royal."

The loop of a lariat settled over Alex's shoulders, imprisoning his arms. Emilio was on the other end of the rope. Dan snatched the pistol from Alex's holster and tossed it aside. Alex fought fiercely, but Dan and Emilio dragged him from the horse and pinned him down.

Kathleen came running. "Get more rope!" Dan panted.

They tied the raving, frothing Alex, hand and foot, carried him into the house and lashed him to a heavy bedstead in a rear room.

"I'll pay you for this, Briscoe," he said, ashen-lipped. "You too, Emilio. I thought you, at least, was my friend."

"And I have proved that I am, *amigo*," Emilio said. "I theenk I have helped save your life."

"Turn him loose after he cools down," Dan told Kathleen after they had moved out of Alex's hearing.

"Is it now that I should go to town to notify them that the *patron* has been murdered?" Emilio asked.

"I'll go," Dan said. "You stay here and stand guard."

He saw apprehension leap into Kathleen's face. Before she could speak, he walked out of the house to his horse.

Just as she had suspected, he had another destination in mind before riding to Flat Butte. Notifying the sheriff and coroner could wait, for the moment at least. Neither of them could bring Bill Royal back to life.

He left the trail a mile from Royal House, and headed west. Cutting across the bend of the river, he passed Shacktown at a distance. Although the hour was still early, only a few lights showed among the scatter of habitations.

He warily approached the gate in the line fence, halting his horse at intervals to listen. He watched the ears of his mount in the starlight, trusting it to scent any horse that might be carrying a rider who was waiting in ambush. But the animal plodded stolidly ahead. The night remained silent as they passed the cattle guard.

An old moon, yellow with time, cleared the rims while the horse was making its way up the long slant toward the ridge that linked the two buttes. Reaching the summit, Dan could make out the buildings of the sheep ranch on the flat below.

A woman's voice, shrill with tension, spoke from the dark brush back of him. "All right, you! Lift your arms! High! I've got you skylined, and I'll shoot if you try to pull a gun. Don't turn around."

The voice belonged to Lavinia Shannon. Dan realized that his horse must have followed some natural route to the summit that other animals had used—a path that was being guarded against intruders by the Shannons.

He lifted his arms. "I'm not carrying a gun," he said. "I'm Dan Driscoll."

"Better known as Diamond Dan Briscoe," she said.

"News *does* travel fast in this range," he commented.

"A man from town came by at dark to warn us," she said.

"That was right friendly of him," Dan remarked. "But, warn you of what?"

"Which one of us did Bill Royal send you over here tonight to kill? Me? Heber? Maybe both of us."

"Is that why you were out here? Waiting for me?"

"That's right. And keep your arms up. I'm not fool enough to believe you haven't got a gun on you. Get down off that horse, slow and careful, then—"

"What if I told you that Bill Royal didn't send me here?" Dan asked. "That would be impossible. Bill Royal is dead."

He heard her draw a sharp, startled breath. There was a space of silence. "Are you lying?" she finally said. "Of course you are. When did he die?"

"A few minutes after your two gunhands stampeded the jag of cattle we had gathered for market. That was just after dark. While we were milling around out there one of them rode to the ranch and shot Bill Royal in the back of the head."

Again the long silence. "Is that the truth?" she demanded.

"That's the reason I rode over here," Dan said. "I wanted to see if all the Shannons were accounted for."

"All the Shannons?" she jeered bitterly. "That means myself and Heber, and my little grandson. We're the only Shannons left. Did you expect my husband and my poor, dead son, Abel, to rise from their graves and be here tonight?"

"Heber's the one I wanted to check up on. Where's he been tonight?"

"I see what you mean. Heber's been at the ranch all night, asleep I hope. He's been working night and day since the pileup, skinning and curing pelts to save what pennies we could."

"Do you know the real names of the men who call themselves Tom Smith and Jim Martin?"

"Why should I?"

"Kathleen Royal thinks you hired them to pose as squatters."

Lavinia Shannon laughed scornfully. "The first thing a guilty person tries to do is point the finger at someone else. We Shannons do our own fighting. We don't hire dirty, night-riding whelps who live in Shacktown."

"Then who does?"

"There's no need to answer that. The same one who's paying you."

"I saw your supply wagon in Flag a few days ago," Dan said. "Wasn't that quite a piece to haul flour and bacon when Obie Willit's store is so handy in Flat Butte?"

"What's it to you as to where we buy our grub, Mr. Diamond Dan Briscoe?"

"Could it be that Obie won't carry you on his credit books any longer?" Dan asked. "And, with all the bad luck you've been having, you're likely mortgaged mighty heavy at the bank. I noticed that Obie is president of the bank, which means that he owns it and that Sid Kain is only his errand boy. I just bet the bank is refusing to extend time on—"

He broke off. "Look!" he exclaimed.

Flames were bursting from one of the buildings at the sheep ranch. Dan heard the distant, heavy slam of a six-shooter. Lavinia Shannon uttered a scream of terror. Dan lowered his arms and looked over his shoulder. She had been standing back of him during their conversation, holding a rifle. The rifle was drooping as she stared, frozen, at the flames in the distance.

"Take my hand," Dan said, for he had not obeyed her command to dismount. "Swing up back of me."

"I've got a horse staked out in the brush," she quavered.

"There's no time for that," Dan said. He lifted her bodily onto the horse, and she clutched his shoulders as he headed the animal at a gallop down the long slant. The distance was more than a mile. The fire was devouring the structure.

"It's the shearing shed," Lavinia Shannon breathed.

The blaze lighted the ranchyard. A small figure had appeared from the ranchhouse and was moving around aimlessly.

"Chad!" Lavinia Shannon screamed. "Chad! Go back! Go back!"

She was shouting futilely at that distance, with the roar of the flames helping drown out her voice. Another frame structure was beginning to burn by the time they reached the ranchyard. It appeared to be a lambing shed that was not being used at this season.

The night had been calm, but the flames were creating their own windstorm, and other buildings as well as the main house might soon be involved.

Dan pulled the horse to a halt. Lavinia Shannon slid to the ground and raced to the small boy, in nightdress, who stood terrified and weeping.

"Chad?" She choked. "Where's your uncle?"

The lad was too terrified to answer. He clung to his grandmother, wailing. Dan swung down and ran closer to the burning shearing shed. A man's body, face-down, was lying almost within reach of the furnace heat from the blaze.

He jammed his hat over his face for protection and did

not dare breathe. Reaching the fallen man, he seized him by an arm and dragged him away from the flames.

The roof of the long shed fell in, its walls collapsing, sending a volcanic gust of fire and smoke into the sky. Dan had the terrible fear his flesh was being cooked as he fought his way out of danger with his burden.

Lavinia Shannon arrived and helped carry the limp form to safer distance. "Heber!" she said in a grief-broken voice. "My son! The last of them. And now they've murdered him too! Curse all the Royals! I'll kill them with my own hands!"

Heber Shannon was not dead. He was breathing, and began to moan. His hair and brows were singed away, but Dan believed he had not been too seriously burned.

But, blood was staining the ground from a wound in his side. "He's been shot!" Dan said.

Two of the Basque herders came riding into the yard, bareback on harness horses. "Try to save the house!" Lavinia shouted at them. "Heber's been shot. I'll look after him."

The Basques began carrying water from the nearby pond, drenching the walls and roof of the main house, which Dan believed was now out of danger. He lifted Heber Shannon in his arms and carried him into the house. Lavinia Shannon lighted a lamp and led the way to a bedroom where she threw back the quilts. Dan placed his burden on the sheet.

Heber Shannon's burns appeared to be superficial, thanks, no doubt, to the bullet that had flattened him face-down on the ground. Dan's own burns were probably more painful.

The bullet wound was something else. It had torn an ugly furrow along Heber Shannon's left side. Lavinia Shannon now moved and worked with icy efficiency. She evidently was no stranger to the sight of blood, and was experienced in the frontier methods of treating injuries.

She paused long enough to turn to Dan. "Go out and tell Bernardo to ride to town and fetch Doc Anderson," she said. *"Muy pronto!"*

Dan complied. Another Basque had arrived and joined the water brigade. Dan seized a tub and helped also. Their efforts succeeded. They prevented further spread of the flames. The shearing shed and the second structure were beyond aid, and Dan finally returned to the house, leaving the debris of these two buildings to burn out.

Heber Shannon was mumbling and throwing off the shock of the bullet wound. He recognized his mother. Then he recognized Dan. That confused him. He kept trying to talk.

Dan bent close. "Who shot you?" he asked.

Heber Shannon tried several times, but could not form words. He lapsed back into a stupor of pain. Dan straightened and moved back.

"You're burned, too," Lavinia Shannon said. "Sit in that chair."

She stripped away Dan's charred shirt. "I don't believe it's too bad," she said, after a moment. "But that left shoulder is going to blister and hurt like the devil for a spell."

She applied a cooling ointment and swathed his left shoulder in a loose bandage. She brought a shirt to replace the one that had been destroyed. "You and my sons are all about the same size," she said.

Dan felt better. He glimpsed himself in a mirror. His brows and eyelashes were almost nonexistent. "I won't take any beauty prizes for a while, at least," he said.

"You saved Heber's life," she said slowly. "I don't understand."

"Understand what?"

"Why did you risk being burned to death to help us?"

"You mean I could have earned my money a lot easier by letting him die?"

Lavinia Shannon was no longer the steel-willed frontier woman. She was a frightened grandmother, bewildered and terrorized. "I don't know what I mean," she sobbed. "I don't know what to think, or how to fight this."

"Maybe I do," Dan said. There was nothing more he could do here. The Basque who had been sent to fetch the doctor should be well on his way to Flat Butte by this time.

Dan walked through the living room. Little Chad Shannon sat huddled in a big chair, frightened, but trying to be brave. Dan patted his head. "He'll be all right soon, sonny," he said. "You can see him before long."

He left the house. The two sheds were slag heaps of blazing beams and crimson ashes. One of the Basques came running, a pistol in one hand, a dirk in the other. He placed the point of the dirk against Dan's chest.

"Ees he dead?" he demanded. He was blackened by smoke, and soaked in sweat. "Eef he die, then you die."

Dan pushed the dirk aside. "He's alive. And I am not the one who shot him."

He walked to his horse and mounted. He had judged his man correctly. Despite his fury, the Basque was not the kind to shoot a man down in cold blood.

Leaving the sheep ranch behind, bathed in the glow of the fading flames, Dan crossed the hogback. The moon was now high in the sky. In its light, he saw the shadow of a moving rider against the pale background of a sand flat a considerable distance away.

Keeping to cover, Dan rode fast, circling ahead of his quarry, which he believed was heading for Spanish Bell territory. When he felt sure he was successful in his plan, he swung back toward the river and waited in the protection of brush.

Luck was with him. The rider's approach carried him within a dozen yards. The mounted man was Alex Emmons.

Dan spoke. "It's Briscoe, Emmons."

He rode into the open. He was covered by Alex's pistol which had been jerked instantly from its holster.

"Seems to me you were supposed to be kept cooped up at Spanish Bell," Dan said.

"Nobody coops me up," Alex snapped. "Why are you skulking around in sheep country?"

Dan didn't speak for a time, while he mulled it over in his mind. He had left Alex tied up at Royal House, but Kathleen, no doubt, had pitied him and had soon turned him loose. Dan had traveled leisurely in his ride toward the Shannon ranch, where he had intended to have a talk with Lavinia Shannon and her son and to present some facts he had put together. It was possible that Alex, knowing the country better, could have ridden to the Shannon place ahead of him.

Dan jerked a thumb over his shoulder in the direction of the sullen red glow in the sky. "It's dangerous to play with matches, Emmons," he said.

"If you're trying to say I touched off that wool ranch,

you're mistaken," Alex said coldly. "It was the fire that brought me here for a look-see."

"And when the sheep were piled up, it was your horse they found," Dan said. "Let's take a look at that rifle you've got slung on your hull. And at the short gun."

"To hell with you," Alex said. Then he had a second thought. "Why?"

"You'd hardly have had the chance to clean the powder smell out of a barrel."

Alex was silent for a space. "That must mean somebody has been shot. Who?"

"Heber Shannon. There was no way of telling whether he was hit by a rifle slug, or one from a six-gun." He waited for some reaction from Alex, but when there was none, added. "The same man who fired that shot must have been the one who set fire to the ranch."

"Is Heber Shannon dead?"

"No. At least, he was alive when I last saw him."

"You were there? At the sheep ranch?"

"Heber was left to die in the fire. I dragged him out."

He added, "I believe Heber knows who shot him. That man better not be in this country if he lives to come after him."

"Meanin' me?"

"What you really rode over here for was to square up for Bill Royal's murder, wasn't it?" Dan said. "You headed this way *before* you saw the glow of the fire, didn't you? Maybe you went to Shacktown first. But Shep Sand and Gid Marko weren't at home. Lucky for you. So you kept going. You aimed to have it out with the Shannons."

"You ought to be a mind reader," Alex said grimly. "You're good at it."

Dan kneed his horse into motion. "Where are you going?" Alex demanded.

"Maybe as far as Flat Butte," Dan said. "I just had a new thought. At least as far along the trail as needed to meet this doctor who acts as coroner. Lavinia Shannon sent a rider to fetch him so he could doctor Heber. He ought to be on his way by this time."

Alex rode at his side. "What's goin' on in this damned country?" Alex said exhaustedly. "Why did the Shannons go wolf? They was friends of the Royals. Why, me an' Heber used to hell around in town together on pay nights. We was pals. Now you think I tried to murder him."

They rode in silence after that. When they reached the cattle guard in the line fence Dan dismounted and began striking matches. He examined the ground on either side of the guard. The trail his own horse had made a few hours earlier was still sharp. So were the hoofmarks of the animal Alex was riding. There was no other sign that any rider had passed this way.

"Is there any other way to cross this fence?" Dan asked.

"There's another gate and cattle guard, but it's an hour's ride south," Alex said.

"How about toward the river?"

"That's only about half a mile. You'd have to cut wire to get through, or risk gettin' bogged down, tryin' to swim a horse around where the fence extends into the water."

Dan mounted and rode along the fence toward the river. They were nearly to the stream when he pulled up. Ahead, the barbed wire dangled loosely from post to post in the moonlight. Two shod horses had entered Shannon range through the cut in the wire—and had returned. The hoofmarks were very fresh.

Dan mounted again without a word, and they headed down the river. They passed Shacktown, which still lay unlighted and apparently asleep. No sound came. Not even a dog barked.

When they reached the fork in the trail, Dan spoke. "Go back to Spanish Bell, Emmons. Stay with Kathleen. Never leave her alone again. Both you and Emilio stand guard until I come back."

"You think the Shannons might try to kill even Katey? A woman?"

"Now which of the Shannons would likely do a thing like that?" Dan asked.

He left Alex and rode off, heading down the trail toward Flat Butte.

CHAPTER ELEVEN

It was scarcely more than an hour before first daybreak when the lights that still burned in Flat Butte appeared ahead. Dan had encountered no traveler on the ride, but he now heard hoofs and the creak of a carriage approaching.

A top buggy loomed up, accompanied by a rider whose tasseled cap identified him as the Basque who had ridden for help.

Dan halted the carriage and rode alongside, peering at the driver. "You're Dr. Anderson, I take it," he said. "Bound for the Shannon place?"

"That's it," the medic said testily. "An' trying to catch me a little sleep on the way. I was fetchin' a pair of twins into this cussed world out at Lang's roadhouse when this Basque fellow found me. Who'n blazes are you?"

"After you get through at the Shannon ranch, go over to Spanish Bell," Dan said. "Bill Royal's been murdered. I understand you serve as coroner in these parts."

"Bill Royal? Gawdalmighty! Heber Shannon shot, and now Bill Royal dead. I knew it'd wind up like this if they didn't come to their senses."

"Who?"

"The Royals and the Shannons, that's who. It'll be a blessing when they wipe each other out, and we don't have any more shootings in the basin to wake a man up in the dead of night."

"What about the sheriff?" Dan asked. "Has anyone—?"

"The Basque here, routed out Art Casey, who's the telegraph operator, and had him get on the line to Flag. It'll be a day or so before the sheriff can get down here. The county can't afford to keep a man on full pay in the basin."

Dan moved his horse out of the way. "Make tracks," he said. "Heber Shannon looked like he could use some help."

He had one more question, and addressed it to the Basque. "Did you see anyone else on your way here?"

"No, señor," the man said. "Not anyone at all."

Dan watched the carriage and the horseman vanish into the run of the trail. Then he rode off the beaten path and circled to the north side of town. He dismounted, tethering the horse in the shadows of timber, and moved in on foot.

The lights of Flat Butte that had blazed so brightly against the brooding blackness of the land when seen at a distance, dwindled to a few, feeble, scattered beams at close range—a phenomenon of the open spaces that never varied.

A lantern glowed in the tunnel of the livery barn. Night lamps burned in Obediah Willit's Great Southwestern Mercantile and in Mack's Place. El Cantina and all other stores were dark. A baby cried in a home where light showed. He heard sleepers snoring in houses as he made his way into the heart of the settlement.

He walked in the powdery dust of the wheel tracks for the sake of silence, and the moon looked down on him. He felt cold fear, for he was an easy target for anyone who might have reason to kill him. He had no alternative. He was taking another step to prove a theory he was evolving.

Flat Butte's main length was that of six average town blocks, with more than half of the frontage vacant and weed-grown. Four or five of the more prosperous citizens had built their homes beyond the east fringe of town in an area where pines grew thinly. The most pretentious of these was a residence built in the ranch style, with adobe, whitewashed walls, a tile roof and tile-floored gallery.

Light seeped from around a curtained window in this house. There was a stone carriage step along the clay sidewalk, with a hitching post formed in the shape of a race jockey, whose left hand held a metal sign which bore the name, Obediah Willit.

Dan silently vaulted the low, white picket fence and made his way nearer the rambling residence. He was sure there was muted talk going on back of the curtained windows—but so cautious were the speakers it could have been that he was only imagining the sounds.

The night held the acrid scent of lathered horses and cooling saddle leather. He moved to the rear of the house where a stable stood. Its double carriage doors were open. He moved a step at a time across a graveled driveway to the opening.

A top buggy, with shafts elevated, occupied the foreground. Dan moved inside the stable. In the faint light that came through the carriage door he made out three horses in the unpaved stock section of the stable. Two of the animals still bore saddles. The third horse had been unrigged and turned into a box stall. It was evident all three had been over a fast trail recently.

He retreated to a hiding place from which he could watch the house. It seemed to him the voices were now raised in anger, but he still could not make out the words. Finally, a rear door opened. The light inside had been snuffed. All he could make out were moving shadows.

Saddle leather creaked. Weary horses drew slobbering sighs of protest. Two men rode out of the stable. They passed close to where he crouched, and were outlined against the sky. One was the bulky Shep Sand. His companion was Gideon Marko.

The night swallowed them. They evidently avoided the heart of the settlement as they rode out of town. Dan felt sure they were heading for Shacktown.

He returned to his horse, mounted and retraced his own route down the trail. He held to a slow pace, not wanting to overtake Sand and Marko in case they were using this same road.

Although daybreak was not far away, Kathleen and Alex were awake and waiting at Royal House. They came to meet him as he dismounted.

"Where in hell have you been?" Alex raged.

"Collecting more saddle blisters," Dan said.

"What have you been up to, Briscoe? We've been waiting for you all night."

"*Mister* Briscoe to you," Dan said.

"Never mind that! What about Doc Anderson? He's never shown up."

"He'll be along, I told him he was more needed at the Shannon ranch."

"That still don't explain why you've been gone for hours. It's four o'clock in the mornin'."

Dan spoke to Kathleen. "Who lives in a dobe-built house on the east end of town? Place is well kept up, with a stable at back."

"That would be Obie Willit's house," she said.

"I just wanted to make sure," Dan said. "His name was on the hitch post. It's a real nice place."

"Who cares about that?" Alex fumed.

"You must be tired, Daniel," Kathleen spoke. "I've had Josefa fix a bed for you in the house. There are plenty of

112

rooms. You'll be more comfortable than in the bunkhouse."

Dan thought of the thick walls of the ranchhouse. "You've made your point," he said. He would at least be more safe, he believed, even though Bill Royal's life had been taken behind these heavy walls so recently. Or so long ago. He was losing track of time.

He walked alone into the big main room, where candles burned. Bill Royal's body lay on an improvised bier beneath a brocaded cloth. The candles stood in tall, silver holders.

Dan removed his hat. He heard Kathleen enter the room and pause. "I'm sorry," he said to her. "Sorry I had no time to learn to know him better."

He regretted speaking, for that shattered the iron composure she had maintained. She began to sob heartbrokenly. Josefa, in nightgown and wrapper, came into the room, took her in her arms, speaking soothingly in Spanish and led her away.

Alex Emmons appeared. "How much do you think she can take, Mister Briscoe?" he said accusingly. His own voice was blurred, his eyes misty. He was trying to fight off tears.

"My name is Daniel," Dan said gently. "Dan to you. All my friends call me that, Alex. I'm proud to know you."

Alex turned and walked out of the room. But not in anger. To hide the grief he could no longer hold back.

"I weel take care of your horse, señor," Emilio said. "You must be very, very tired. You must sleep."

Dan nodded. He stood alone for a moment longer, looking down at the figure on the bier. The highboy Bill Royal had been trying to reach when death had overtaken him stood nearby. He walked to it and opened the drawer whose handle the rancher had been clutching when the bullet had struck him.

He stood looking at what the drawer contained. Two holstered pistols and a gunbelt. Fine weapons and fine leather. His guns. The three-hundred-dollar matched set he had abandoned at Yellow Lance the night he had tried to cast aside the past and begin a new life.

The past was alive again. He was seeing a drink-maddened man go down before these guns. And seeing the other two who had faced these weapons. Above all, he was seeing Frank Buckman stride to his death.

He turned. Kathleen had returned and had been watching. She spoke. "I brought them from Yellow Lance. John Cass gave them to me. I—I thought you might need them again. At that time I didn't know you. I do now. You don't need those pistols. Ever."

Dan gazed at the guns for a long time. Then he pushed the drawer shut. Silently, she led him through the house to a bedroom where a lamp burned. "Good night," she said. "Alex and Emilio will stand watch. It's daybreak. Sleep in peace."

No phantoms came to torment him. It was nearly noon when he awakened. He could hear voices in the house. He dressed hastily, and walked to the living room.

A craggy-faced man he realized must be the doctor from Flat Butte was talking to Kathleen and Alex Emmons.

"Good morning," Dan said. "You're Dr. Anderson, I take it. I'm the one who met you on the trail last night. How did things come out at the Shannon place?"

"Not so good," the medic said. He was unshaven, his shoulders sagging with weariness.

"Heber Shannon is in very bad shape," Kathleen said.

Dan looked at the doctor. "You mean he's dying? That there's no hope?"

The doctor was irritable with frustration and exhaustion. "Everybody asks that. How in hell do I know? He may pull out of it, he may not."

"Get the doctor a drink, Kathleen," Dan said. "A slug of whiskey. A solid slug."

She hurried away, returning with a bottle and glasses. The doctor tossed off a drink, wagged his head and attempted a smile. "It's one medicine I never prescribe, but it might be the cure for me right now."

He added, "If only I could help Lavinia. There's the one who's suffering. A husband, a son in their graves. Now another son."

"Can Heber Shannon talk?" Dan asked.

Dr. Anderson gave him a searching look. "I believe you had better ask someone else that question. Lavinia, for instance."

He relented a trifle. "Heber did no talking while I was

114

there. I had to put him under while I probed for the bullet."

"You got the bullet out? What was it? Could you tell the caliber?"

"That," the doctor said grimly, "is for the sheriff to decide. I'll hand it over to him when he shows up. He should arrive by tomorrow at the latest."

He turned to leave. "I've other patients to visit," he said. "I'll go back to the Shannon place as soon as possible. Tomorrow, I hope. Baldy seems to be doing all right. I'm no longer needed here."

"How about the one in there?" Dan demanded, indicating the room where the candles burned. "That's a matter for the sheriff too. And also the coroner. I believe you're the coroner."

"I'll call an inquest tomorrow," the doctor snapped.

"A waste of time," Kathleen said bitterly. "We know what the verdict will be. Cause of death—a bullet, fired either accidentally, or by a person unknown. That's the only verdict any of your juries ever bring in Springwater Basin these days."

"Good day!" Dr. Anderson said stiffly, and stalked out of the house to his carriage. He drove hurriedly away, evidently determined to be neutral.

"And he used to be such a good friend," Kathleen said despondently.

CHAPTER TWELVE

The funeral was delayed until sundown the following day, for Kathleen wanted to allow time for friends to arrive and pay their respects. However, only a handful turned up. All were men, mainly town folk, along with two ranchers who operated small outfits north of the basin.

Obie Willit came into the ranchyard at the last minute in his varnished top buggy. The minister delayed opening the services until the storekeeper had paid his respects to Kathleen.

"Sorry I'm late, Katey," Willit said, taking both her

hands. "I can't tell you how hard hit I was by the news. If there's anything I can do to help you bear up under this great loss, all you have to do is let me know."

Kathleen withdrew her hands. "Please start the services," she said to the minister.

The grave had been dug by Alex and Emilio on a tree-shaded site, alongside the burial place of Kathleen's mother. They had refused all help. Dan had respected their wishes, knowing they felt this was about the only way they could show Bill Royal how they felt.

The sermon was dull and sonorous. And meaningless. Dan saw that the man was avoiding any word that might offend a listener. Like all the others, he was trying to be carefully neutral.

"Amen!" Kathleen said sharply, halting the sermon abruptly.

After a moment of confusion, a hymn was started by a nasal-voiced woman, who was the wife of the minister. Alex Emmons halted her also. Alex and Emilio and Josefa finished the hymn in unison, their voices deepened by the intensity of their feelings.

Dan stepped forward, recited the Lord's Prayer, and consecrated Bill Royal's body to the earth. The casket, made of native wood, which Alex and Emilio had shaped with their own hands, was sprinkled with dust. The final amens were said.

The mourners began to stream toward their equipages after the casket was lowered. Dan waited, intending to help with filling the grave.

A spring wagon with a team in harness came into the ranchyard, the horses at a run, with two men on the seat. The men alighted and walked toward the thinning group at the grave. Both wore badges on their vests.

"Which one of you is a man who calls himself Dan Driscoll an' is better known as Daniel Briscoe?" the bigger of the two, who wore the star of a sheriff, asked.

"I'm Dan Briscoe," Dan spoke.

Sheriff Ben Hughes and his deputy strode to his side. Before Dan realized their intention, he found himself linked by handcuffs to the two officers, one on either side.

"You're under arrest," the sheriff said, enjoying this moment of dramatic importance in front of so many citizens.

"For what?" Dan demanded.

"Murder! What else?"

"Murder? Whose murder?"

"As if you didn't know," the officer snorted. "You bushwhacked Heber Shannon, then set fire to the ranch to cover the crime."

Dan was dumfounded. "Heber Shannon is dead?" he asked.

"That's right, and you'll likely hang for it. The citizens of this county are mighty sick of the likes of you, and the killings that have gone on in this basin."

"But Lavinia Shannon, herself, can tell you I *couldn't* have shot Heber," Dan said. "I was talking to her at the time."

"Now that makes me laugh," the officer jeered. "It just happens that it was Livvy Shannon, herself, who signed the affidavit, namin' you as the man. She was waitin' for me when I pulled into Flat Butte a little while ago. She saw you shoot her son. Saw you with her own eyes."

The officers began crowding him toward their wagon. He was too stunned to resist. "Lavinia Shannon wouldn't say that!" he protested. "She couldn't!"

"Well she could an' did. Step lively now."

Kathleen seized the sheriff's arm. "You're wrong! Dan Briscoe doesn't even carry a gun!"

"My advice to you is to keep out o' this, Miss Royal," the sheriff said. "Everybody knows you hired this man to come here. Everybody knows he's a killer. He's Diamond Dan Briscoe, who used to wear a badge as an excuse to shoot people."

"How did you learn that?" Dan asked.

"Everybody in Flat Butte knows it," the sheriff said, still addressing Kathleen. "There's such a thing as being accessory to murder. I never yet had to put a woman in jail on a charge like that, an' I'd dislike havin' to make you the first one, Katey. I knew your father. If I can get proof you paid blood money to Diamond Dan Briscoe it'll be my duty to see that you stand trial."

"What about the gunmen Lavinia Shannon has brought into the basin?" Kathleen demanded. "What about Tom Randall's murder? What about my riders being beaten and terrorized until I can't get a crew together to round up enough beef to keep Spanish Bell going?"

"I tried my best to get evidence as to who killed Tom

117

Randall," the sheriff said defensively. "The same as I tried to find out who killed Livvy Shannon's son, Abel."

"What about my father? We just buried him with a bullet in his brain. Did Livvy Shannon say she saw that murder, too? Of course not. She only sent the killer here to pull the trigger. She—"

"Don't you go making wild charges you can't back up," the sheriff warned. "I promise I'll do my best to bring to justice whoever shot your father. If you got any evidence that'll help, I'll listen to it. I'm stayin' in this country to look into it. This fight between you Royals an' the Shannons is a crime an' a shame. Good men killed because two families turned into hogs an' wanted to bite off more'n they can chew."

"That's a lie, Ben Hughes. The Shannons are the ones who set out to ruin us. They've about succeeded, but I'm still alive and still have title to Spanish Bell. They'll never get their hands on it if there's any mortal way I can prevent it."

The sheriff sighed. "Jed. Take the prisoner into town. An' see to it that he don't get away—alive."

Dan was prodded at gunpoint into the wagon. The sheriff handcuffed him to the iron support that fringed the back of the seat.

The officer turned to Obediah Willit, who stood among the onlookers. "I reckon I'll have to lock him up in your root cellar at the store, Obie," he said, "bein' as the county's still too poor to build a calaboose in Flat Butte. I'll take him to Flag next stage run."

Obie Willit shrugged. "I don't hanker at havin' my place used as a jail, but you're the law, Ben. Here's a key to the back door. I'll be along later. I want to talk to Katey."

"I want to talk to her some more myself," the sheriff said. "I'll see you tomorrow, Jed."

The deputy, a gangling man with an active Adam's apple, climbed in beside Dan and freed the reins from the whip socket. "Mister," he said ominously, "I'll put a slug in your brisket if'n you try a wrong move. You kin take Jed Jenkins' word for that. I got no likin' fer killers."

Kathleen came to the side of the vehicle. "I'll hire a lawyer," she told Dan. "I'll try to raise bail. I'll make Livvy Shannon admit she's lying."

His arrest had seemed so unreal that Dan had been unable to believe it was actually happening until this moment. The sheriff was mistaken, of course, about Lavinia Shannon accusing him of shooting her son. Why, she had even seen him drag Heber Shannon away from the flames. There had been gratitude in Livvy Shannon, not accusation.

Or *were* they mistaken?

Dan looked back as the deputy headed the team up the trail toward Flat Butte. Alex Emmons stood alone, his face shadowed by his hat. Dan was remembering that Alex had refused to let his guns be examined after Heber Shannon had been shot.

"I'm watchin' you every second, big man," Jed Jenkins warned as the wagon bounced across the irrigation bridge.

A mile later, Jenkins spoke again, "Maybe you might figure a bullet would be an easy way out. Let me tell you that I never let 'em take a prisoner away from me yet, but there might be a first time."

"Say that again, and clearer," Dan demanded.

"Folks in Flat Butte was right worked up when we pulled in there this afternoon," Jenkins said. "They'd jest heard about this Heber Shannon bein' shot, an' Bill Royal murdered. They were allowin' that they was tired o' paid killers bushwhackin' people. They said they'd make an example o' the first one they got their hands on."

Dan said nothing. The handcuffs became very real, very cold on his wrists. He tested their strength. They were unyielding. He cautiously slid the metal links along the curved steel rod. The rod was solidly moored to the seat of the wagon. There was no hope in that direction.

Dusk came, and the soft mountain darkness was closing in as Jenkins sent the team along at a fast clip. The man sat stiff and alert, staying as far away from Dan as possible. He was jumpy. The flight of an owl overhead caused him to jerk his six-shooter from its holster. He did not begin breathing normally for some time. After that, he kept the gun in his lap.

He swung the rig off the trail. The vehicle lurched over brush and rough ground through scattered timber. The lights of Flat Butte appeared. Jenkins circled the town in order to approach it from the north.

He finally halted the team. "All right," he said, alighting

and tethering the animals. "We'll injun in. If you start a scuffle, what happens will be on your own haid."

He freed Dan's hands from the rod, but linked their wrists together with one manacle. Picking a route through the back lanes, he prodded Dan ahead with the muzzle of his gun, until they reached the rear of the bulky mercantile building.

The key Obediah Willit had given the officers opened a rear door and they moved inside. A night lamp burned, but the blinds on the front window were not drawn and the store was exposed to the street.

Dan had believed Jenkins' wariness was only a pose, intended to frighten him, rather than due to any real fear of a lynching attempt. He was wrong.

A shout arose in the street. "There they air! Snuck in from the back!"

That voice belonged to Shep Sand. Others joined in. "Murderer! Dirty killer!"

Apparently the group had been waiting for some time, watching the store.

"Them fellers mean business!" Jenkins chattered. "I'm tellin' you one thing, Briscoe, I ain't gittin' myself killed by tryin' to save your neck."

A rock smashed a front window. "Come on!" a man roared. "Let's string him up, here an' now. It'll save the county the expense of a trial."

An unshaven, frightened face appeared above a counter. Jenkins swung his six-shooter around. "Don't shoot!" the owner of the face croaked. "It's only me, Link Hoffer, the cleanup man. I sleep here at nights."

Link Hoffer headed for the rear door to escape. "You better come with me, shurruf," he wheezed. "Them are tough customers out there. They ain't town folk. They're them squatters from Shacktown. They came into town before sundown, an' have been drinkin' an' makin' ugly talk ever since."

Hands began to shake the front door. Link Hoffer stampeded out of the building. Jed Jenkins suddenly produced a key and freed Dan from the handcuff.

"Run fer it!" Jenkins panted. "I'm givin' you a chance."

Jenkins started to follow Link Hoffer's example, and head for the rear door, to escape.

Dan seized him by the arm. "No you don't, you gopher!" he snapped. "You know they'll blast me down!"

He tore the pistol from Jenkins' hand, and sent the man sprawling on the floor with a shove. The deputy crawled to the shelter of a counter.

The front door crashed open. Dan vaulted over a counter and used it as a breastwork. "I'm here!" he shouted. "And armed. Who'll be the first to ask for a slug in the belly? I can take care of at least five of you."

Shep Sand's beefy figure had appeared in the wide doorway. At his shoulder was Gid Marko. They halted!

"Hello, Shep!" Dan said. "I figured you had rounded up this lynching party. This is Dan Briscoe from Yellow Lance. I believe you've heard of me."

Sand and Marko vanished from the opening. Their heads appeared briefly a moment later at the corners of windows on either side of the door.

"All right, boys!" Sand shouted. "Go in and get him! We'll smoke him up, so he can't do any shooting."

Nobody moved. "Go git him yoreself, Smith!" someone jeered. "You been actin' like Billy Big. Let's see you walk in there."

"He's all alone!" Sand yelled. "Are you going to let one man bluff out the lot of you?"

A woman's voice sounded shrilly. "No lynching! No lynching! Not that! Dear God, not that!"

The speaker was Lavinia Shannon. She was hatless, her gray hair unkempt, her face drawn. She pushed through the crowd and appeared in the doorway.

Another voice spoke angrily, "Livvy! Don't be a fool! This is no place fer you! Go on back to your ranch."

Obediah Willit plowed his way to Livvy Shannon's side. Evidently he had just arrived from Spanish Bell, for he still carried a buggy whip in his hand.

At almost the same moment Dan heard more persons enter the store by the rear door. He swung his pistol around. But the ones who had arrived were Kathleen Royal and Alex Emmons. Kathleen carried a rifle in her hands. Alex had a brace of six-shooters in his fingers, the hammers cocked. They moved to his side.

Lavinia Shannon was speaking again. "Don't bring the wrath of God on our heads by hanging a man without a fair trial. Let the law take care of this."

"Of all people, Livvy, you ought to be the last to help this killer," Obie Willit thundered. "You saw him shoot down your son in cold blood, saw it with your own eyes. That's the truth, ain't it?"

Lavinia Shannon did not answer for a space. "Yes!" she said in the same dead voice. "But it's not for a mob to punish the guilty."

It was over. The inflamed lynching spirit had been quenched. "Go back to your homes, citizens," Obie Willit said, as though preaching a sermon. "Livvy's right. This man will be held for trial before a jury of his peers."

He paused for effect, then went on, his big voice rolling through the town. "I promise you he'll see nothin' but prison walls the rest o' his days, an' if Heber Shannon can't make it back to life, this man will hang from a gallows that I'll help build with my own hands. I'll see to it that court is held right here, an' justice done where all citizens of Flat Butte can see the penalty paid."

His voice rose still higher. "An' we will pray that it be a lesson to them that've let greed drive them to war on their neighbors for the sake of adding a few cubits of land to what they already own. If we do not drive these people from our temple, the name of Springwater Basin will become a stench in the land. I say a pox on both of them, even though they are of the so-called gentler sex."

He brought the whip down on the platform with a loud report. "A horsewhippin' might bring 'em to their senses!" he added, bending scowls on both Livvy Shannon and Kathleen Royal.

Kathleen spoke. "I really did misjudge you, Obie. I won't make that mistake again."

"There's no call for lashin' at me, Katey!" the store owner thundered. "Everybody knows you an' Livvy have turned as sour as sin an' as venomous as rattlers. Springwater Basin will be better off without the two of you."

"How could we have been so blind, Livvy?" Kathleen said.

"Let's get out of here," Dan said. He pushed Kathleen toward the rear door. Jed Jenkins crouched there in hiding and made a feeble attempt to intervene.

"Get out of my way, you miserable excuse for a lawman!" Dan said. He placed a boot against the deputy's shoulder and again sent him sprawling.

Followed by Alex, he and Kathleen walked out of the building. A few men stood uncertainly in the darkness, unable to make up their minds whether to interfere. Three saddled horses stood ground-tied near the exit from the store. One had loose stirrups lashed across the saddle.

Dan freed the stirrups. "You came prepared," he said to Kathleen.

"Yes, thanks to Hallie Barnes."

"Hallie Barnes? Who's she?"

"You mean you've forgotten her already? You should be ashamed. She's very grateful to you for pulling her child out of the bog. She came riding to the ranch, not long after the sheriff had left, to tell us that Tom Smith had rounded up half a dozen squatters at Shacktown, got them fired up on liquor, and had led them to town to pull off a lynching. She understood that you were to be the lynchee, as one might put it. Therefore, Alex and myself lit a fast shuck for town to interfere in the proceedings, if possible. But Livvy Shannon had already taken care of the situation."

"My good deed was rewarded," Dan said. "You two know, of course, that the law frowns on people helping prisoners escape. Particularly, prisoners charged with murder."

"So what?" Kathleen sniffed. "Hurry, before some fool starts real trouble."

"Exactly," Dan said. "At least one of that mob isn't a fool. Shep Sand. Gid Marko's there, too. There might be fireworks. And they can shoot."

He lifted her into the saddle. "Stay ahead of us," he commanded as he and Alex mounted.

They spurred away. A voice yelled, "There they go!"

Pistols opened up, but the marksmen had only shadows and the sound of galloping hoofs to guide them, and the firing halted after a few rounds were touched off.

"Are you two all right?" Dan demanded.

"Not a scratch," Alex said. "Where'd they learn to shoot? In a popgun gallery?"

"Something like that," Dan said. "Places like Dodge City. Julesburg. Deadwood. We were lucky."

CHAPTER THIRTEEN

Kathleen led the way. She headed north for two miles or more, then swung directly west.

"You two go back to Royal House," Dan said. "Stay there. See to it that nobody tries to burn you out like someone did the Shannons the other night."

"Someone?" Alex said caustically. "If you're the one that shot Heber Shannon, then you must have set fire to the buildings too, Mister Briscoe."

"I seem to remember that you were skulking around in Shannon range at the time," Dan said.

"But you're the one Livvy Shannon says she saw shoot Heber. Seems like they've got you dead to rights on that, my friend."

"It does, doesn't it?"

Kathleen spoke. "Go to the ranch, Alex. Please."

"And what do you aim to do?"

"Please do as I ask."

"You're going with this fellow, aren't you?" Alex said. There was a sudden, empty despair in his voice.

"I know the country better than he does," she said. "Somebody has to show him where to hide. That deputy likely is already swearing in a posse to hunt him down."

"It'll only go the worse for you if you're caught with him," Alex said. "Even if the law doesn't come down on you, the gossips will."

"To blazes with the gossips."

"Why don't I go with him?" Alex demanded. "I know the country, too."

"That's right," Dan said. "Alex can—"

"I'm already in this up to my chin," she said coolly. "Alex really didn't help you get away from that fool deputy. I did. I own the horse you're riding. In addition, I know a hideout that Alex doesn't know about. A special place."

She rode close to Alex, leaned over and kissed him on the lips. "Alex," she said. "I'm older than you. I know how you feel about me. I love you. I think the world of you. But I don't love you the way you wish."

124

Alex rode in dead silence for a time. When he spoke, he tried to voice it lightly, but that was a failure. His voice was still blurred with the pain and misery of it. "All right, Katey. I'll go to the ranch."

He pulled up and looked at Dan in the pale light of the waning moon. "Why did it have to be you, of all people? She buried one man she intended to marry. Now you come along. You know you won't live long. Maybe not another day. Why bring this on her again?"

He rode away, heading in the direction of Spanish Bell. Kathleen turned her mount westward again. Dan followed.

He knew she was weeping in the darkness of the timber through which they rode, weeping for the loneliness she knew she had brought on a person who was like a brother to her.

"He's right, you know," Dan said at last.

She turned savagely on him. "He doesn't have the right to say things like that. Nor to speak for me."

"He told the truth," Dan said. "You are in love with me. And the chances are I won't be alive very long."

"I only feel responsible for you being here, for getting involved," she said. "I owe it to you to help you all I can."

"Of course," Dan said. "I'm grateful."

"Thank you," she said. "Thank you for understanding me, *Mister* Briscoe."

"The trouble is," Dan said, "that I'm in love with you too."

She would not look at him. She kept riding westward. "Where are we going?" Dan asked gently.

She still did not respond for a time. When she spoke, her voice was still shaking with emotion. She pointed toward Flat Butte and its twin which loomed blackly against the night sky.

"There," she said.

"That's Shannon country."

"Yes."

"We'll be hunted, of course. The deputy had no backbone, but the sheriff looked to me like he was shingled from a different tree. He won't quit, I'd say."

"He's tough," she said. "Ben Hughes will do his best to try to catch us."

"Me—not us," Dan said. "After all, they won't really try to hang a charge on you. That's ridiculous."

When she did not answer, he added. "You must keep out of this. Show me this hideout you mentioned, then go home."

"And let you take the blame for everything?"

It was Dan who had no ready answer for that. They rode steadily for mile after mile without speaking. The horses worked their way up the long ridge between the buttes and crossed the hogback. A light, far away, marked the location of the Shannon ranch. Dan realized they were north of the river, separated from the ranch by the stream's gorge.

They rode through broken country, with rocky bluffs rising to force detours. The horses were slogging it despondently, weary and dispirited. Dan rode lumpily in the saddle. Exhaustion had suddenly descended on him like a heavy weight. Kathleen was slumped also, her hands clamped on the saddlehorn, her head bobbing listlessly.

"Daybreak's near," Dan said thickly. "We better be hanging up soon."

"We're almost there," she answered.

She led the way down a rocky ravine where the horses picked their way gingerly, sparks flying from shod hoofs that slid on hard rock. They leveled off alongside the main river which boiled and fumed over boulders.

Kathleen urged her mount into the margin of the stream, forcing it to endure the rush of the current. "Keep your horse in the water," she said. "We don't want to leave tracks that will tell them which way we went. It'll only be a few more minutes."

The animals floundered over boulders and at times went belly-deep in pools. The going eased. Dan saw that the stream was fringed by a meadow and small sand flats. Dawn was beginning to give some light. Dead ahead they faced what seemed to be an unbroken granite wall that soared two hundred feet or more.

Kathleen forced her unwilling horse ahead. The stream seemed to emerge from the base of the cliff. The depth of the water increased. "Monkey style," she said. She was crouching on her knees on the saddle to stay dry. Dan followed her example.

Blackness loomed ahead. They were enclosed by the

walls of the cliff. He saw that they had entered what seemed to be almost a tunnel, but was in reality a slit, wide at the bottom, with the walls overhanging and narrowing fifty feet or more overhead.

"All right," Kathleen said. The water shallowed. The light strengthened. They emerged on a sandy shore. The river, fifty feet wide, and shallow, slid smoothly past on a rock bottom. Overhead was open sky.

The horses stood spent and blowing. They dismounted. Dan stared at a small, rude shack, built of rocks and driftwood which stood on a sort of rocky ledge above the flood mark of the river. The cliff protected it from the weather.

Kathleen left her horse and climbed the rude steps to the shack. She peered inside the doorless structure.

"We're here," she said with satisfaction. "We'll have shelter, at least. And even food, such as it is. We can unsaddle. No need worrying about the horses. They won't drift away. This has only one entrance. There's enough grass around so they can rustle for themselves."

"You amaze me," Dan said. "Is this a part of some secret outlaw past?"

"A part of the past, at least. I haven't been here in more than two years, I believe it is. Since the trouble with the Shannons began. I used to come here occasionally."

"Why?"

"To fish for trout, sometimes. There are some dandies in that stream. But mainly, just to dream."

"This is the place for it, from the looks," Dan said.

He carried the saddles to the ledge and peered inside the shack. A rude fireplace of rocks, chinked with mud, had its vent against the face of the cliff. There were two bunk frames made of pine poles, slung with cured elkhides.

Daylight was strengthening, revealing that their hideout was a sizable alcove of perhaps three acres. "From the outside the bluff looks solid," Kathleen explained. "This is the real headwater of Springwater River. We found this by luck when we were youngsters while we were trout fishing."

"We?"

"Abel Shannon and myself."

Dan peered at her. "Abel *Shannon?*"

"Yes. I doubt if it would matter even if Abel were alive. This is neutral ground. We took solemn blood oath we would never reveal this to any other person except in dire need."

"How old were you two when you took this pledge?"

"I was about ten, Abel twelve. We were fishing and hunting pals in those days. Heber was more the bookworm type, and considered such things a waste of time. Heber always wanted to go to college and study to be a doctor. I believe he'd have made it if the trouble hadn't started."

She entered the shelter and opened a dust-filmed box made of cedar. It had a brand burned into its lid, an enclosed S. "The Shannon sheep brand," she said. "Circle S."

She drew out blankets, quilts and bed tarps. Delving deeper, she produced canned food and a supply of coffee beans that were stored in an airtight tin.

She carried the bedding into the open and spread it on brush in the sun. "It's all in the best of shape," she said.

"How long did you say it had been since you were here?"

"About two years," she answered. "But Abel must have kept coming here until—until he was killed. That was about a year ago."

"You and Abel Shannon used to camp here together?"

She eyed him, and was suddenly greatly amused. "Why, you're actually shocked. If you must know the bitter truth, even though it crushes my vanity, Abel never looked on me as anything except a sort of *peón* who was only useful at driving deer his way or doing the camp chores. From schooldays, he was in love with the girl he married when he grew up. Her name was Angelina Phillips, from Flat Butte. A pretty redhead."

She was silent for a space. "Angie died when Chad Shannon was born," she went on. "Abel never got over it. After Angie was gone he used to come here more often than before. Not to dream, but to mourn."

"Maybe he told someone else about this place. There would hardly be any point in keeping it secret after you two grew up, especially when the feud started. Maybe he told Heber. Or Livvy Shannon. If so, we can expect the sheriff to drop in with a posse."

"I doubt that. I know it sounds childish, but I believe Abel stood by our pledge. I would have stood by it."

"And if you're wrong . . . ?"

"The Shannons still wouldn't tell the sheriff about this place."

128

"Even though Lavinia Shannon says I shot Heber?"

She eyed him levelly. "She knows you didn't shoot him."

"That means you believe Lavinia is lying."

"Of course. I know Lavinia. Lying comes hard with her. I had the belief she was doing something against her will—against her nature. It was as though she was doing it against her religion, against her God."

"If I didn't shoot Heber, then who did? Do you have any ideas on that?"

"Certainly. Just as you do. One of those two gunmen must have done it. The ones you say are Shep Sand and Gideon Marko."

Dan picked up a tarp and quilt. "I'll bed down somewhere outside," he said.

She halted him. "You think Alex might have shot Heber, don't you?"

"He was over in Shannon range that night."

"When Alex came back to Spanish Bell the night Heber was shot, he asked a strange thing. He asked me to look at his six-shooter and rifle and decide if either had been fired recently. And, if so, if it looked like they had just been cleaned. Neither gun showed any such sign. Alex had Emilio look at them. And even Baldy, who is beginning to be able to get around."

"As a matter of fact I never really believed he did it," Dan admitted. "I only wanted to be positive. He refused to let me look at his guns when I mentioned it. That was his infernal pride."

"So?"

"We're both thinking the same thing," Dan said. "Shep Sand or Marko might have pulled the trigger on Heber Shannon, but someone else paid them to do it. You know who I mean."

"Obie Willit," she said. "Of course."

"How long have you known?" Dan asked.

"I began to really suspect it when he came to my father's funeral and I saw his crocodile tears. It must have been in my mind before that. It suddenly was plain enough. Obie's got such a reputation for honesty, he just kept slipping out of our minds. He owns the bank, and probably will own both Spanish Bell and the Shannon range unless he's stopped."

"Just how deep are you in?"

"We've been staving off foreclosure for months. I'm sure the Shannons are in the same boat."

"How about Shacktown? Was it worth it for him?"

"Yes. Decidedly so. Bringing those squatters in cost him only the price of what food and furniture he gave them. All this talk about a dam being built in the basin, and irrigation coming in, isn't all talk, I'm sure. Obie was spending money to make money. He's got millions in sight if he gets away with it."

"He's spending money, sure enough," Dan commented.

"Shep Sand's price comes high. Marko's, too. I've got a hunch Obie Willit is wishing he'd never heard of those two. It's like the story of the camel getting its head inside the tent. Pretty soon, Obie will find himself out in the cold—and maybe with a bullet in his back, while that pair take over."

"I took it for granted the Shannons were paying them," Kathleen sighed. "I can see now that this belief was hammered into my mind, little by little, by Obie himself. Each time he met me or my father, he would whisper some warning against the Shannons. He pretended he was on the side of Spanish Bell."

"And turning his coat when he talked to the Shannons."

"I'm shamed," she said.

"For what?"

"For letting the wool be pulled over our eyes. Obie's not only a thief. He's a murderer. He was back of every thing that's happened. When did you begin to suspect him?"

"I posed as a man thinking of homesteading. A woman had told me it was easy to get credit at the bank in Flat Butte if you took a claim along the river."

"A woman? A pretty one, I take it?"

"Maybe," Dan said. "I couldn't tell for sure. She needed some soap and water."

Kathleen laughed. Dan told of the episode of the child and the bog hole. "On a hunch, I rode into town, talked to Sid Kain, then laid low to see under which shell I'd find the pea. Kain waited until he believed that I'd left town, then ran like a rabbit to the mercantile. He wanted instructions. I had found my pea. Obie Willit was running the show. Fact is, all signs pointed to him beforehand. What I don't know is how and when he found out I was Dan Briscoe."

"I'm afraid that was another mistake on my part," Kathleen said grimly. "I wrote two letters to Uncle John Cass at Yellow Lance for my father. I made the mistake of mailing them in Flat Butte."

"I guess that would be enough," Dan said. "Obie probably put two and two together, after I showed up. It was in the papers that I had resigned as marshal at Yellow Lance after Frank Buckman and young Hatch were killed."

"Obie's sister-in-law is postmistress in Flat Butte," Kathleen said. "I doubt if Obie even had to read the newspapers. Knowing what we know now, I imagine all our mail was opened and read before it was sent out."

She added angrily, "How stupid could I have been?"

"That's the way it looks now," Dan said. "But Obie worked it smart. If it's any consolation, the Shannons swallowed all the bait too. Up to now, at least."

"Up to now? You mean Lavinia—?"

"I'm sure she's caught on to Obie Willit's scheme, the same as you."

"Then why did she try to have you hung?"

"When the chips were down she rushed in to prevent my neck from being stretched," Dan said. "Remember?"

Kathleen eyed him. "I wonder why?" she said slowly.

"She acted to me like a person caught between two devils," Dan said. "She's in a squeezer, if you ask me, and somebody's twisting the screws."

"Nobody could ever force Lavinia Shannon to do anything against her will," Kathleen said positively. "She's made of steel, that woman."

"The person doesn't live who hasn't got some weak point," Dan said.

"They could burn her with branding irons, tear her apart on the rack. She'd never give in. I know. My father tried to talk sense to her about this feud. I tried."

"Maybe she looks at the Royals the same way. Did you Royals offer anything but threats and accusations?"

Kathleen started a denial, then went silent. "We were in the right," she said weakly.

"And so were the Shannons. You both were in the right. In this case two rights made a wrong."

"I'll never forgive Lavinia," she said. "Not after the way she almost had you lynched. Even though she repented at the last minute, I'll hold it against her. All she had in mind was to discredit Spanish Bell and to turn what few friends we still had in Flat Butte against us."

"You're still letting your temper overcome your judgment," Dan said chidingly. "Who'd benefit by that? Not the Shannons. Obie Willit would be able to take over your outfit that much easier, without being suspected, if you had no friends. Then he'd have the Shannons at his mercy and would soon wipe them out."

"But Lavinia lied when she said you shot Heber."

"Men of steel have been forced to lie at times, against their will. Why not a woman?"

"Forced?"

"Only she can tell us," Dan said. "Maybe tonight."

"Tonight?"

"If the sign is right. But, first of all, let's have a bite of grub and then some sleep. There's little chance of smoke being sighted in this early light. I'm hungry, and could stand some hot coffee."

A coffeepot, a skillet and two blackened, battered metal cooking pots were stored in the shack. Kathleen carried the utensils to the river and washed them while Dan built a small fire of dry twigs that would give little smoke. He pulverized coffee beans in a small grinder which bore Abel Shannon's carved initials. They ate an improvised mixture of canned meat, tomatoes and corn, and drank strong, black coffee.

"Best meal I ever tucked away," Dan said. "And seems like it's about the first in a month or so."

Afterward, he carried his bedding a distance from the shack, and found a place in the shade of willows near the river.

"Good night!" Kathleen called from the shelter. "Or, just what would a person say at this time of day?"

"That will take some thought," Dan answered. Then he slept.

CHAPTER FOURTEEN

It was midafternoon when he awakened. The alcove held drowsy warmth in the cliffs. Jays squawked in the brush and a cicada exploded with its hissing call. He heard the harsh scolding of a squirrel. The inevitable gnat came to dance tantalizingly before his eyes as he sat up.

The stream murmured softly, its surface dark and smooth as it swept toward the exit from the hideout. A trout leaped in the dark shadow of the cliff. Their horses stood knee-deep in the river, tails swinging lazily to baffle the gnats.

Kathleen emerged from the shelter, arranging her hair. Sleep had eased some of the marks of strain and fatigue. "Good afternoon, Daniel," she said. "It seems we've wasted the best hours of the day."

"I never saw a better place for it," Dan said. He eyed the stream and shivered. "I'm going to hate this. That water looks cold. I like my bathtubs hot. But it's necessary. I'll pick that stand of willows downstream for my own."

Kathleen laughed, a clear, warm sound that belonged in this beautiful scene. She seemed surprised by her own lightness of spirit. On the heels of that came contrition. She was remembering her father, and her conscience was accusing her for finding laughter when the soil was so newly turned on his grave.

"You need more laughter, Kathleen," he said. "Bill Royal would be the first to tell you that, if he were here. There's been enough grief to last a lifetime."

He added, "There's a fine screen of brush at the upper end of the pool, which will never be invaded by the eyes of men—at least today, blast my scruples."

He walked away. Once more he heard the laughter. That was the result he had been seeking.

Afterward, he watched Kathleen dry her hair in the sun. She moored it down as best she could with what pins she had managed to save. She walked to the stream, trying to find a reflection clear enough to appraise the result of her efforts.

She sighed, and said, "I must be a sight."

Dan grinned. "I remember hearing my mother say the same thing each time she finished with her hair. Is a woman ever satisfied, after all that fuss and bother?"

"Tell me about your mother," she said.

"That's about all I can remember. She died when I was a small button. So did my father. But I remember watching her comb her hair. It was long and rich. Like your hair."

Color came high in her cheeks. She was pleased. "Tell

me that all this is real," she said softly and swung her arms to encompass their surroundings. "Tell me that the other part of it was the nightmare. Tell me—"

Far away, beyond their walls, three gunshots sounded, evenly spaced. After a moment, three more shots were fired from farther away, for they were very faint.

They remained silent, listening. But, all they could hear was the whispering of the river as it rolled oilily past.

They both knew these were the customary signals by which men kept in touch with each other when separated in rough country. These shots, no doubt, had been fired by hunters. Man-hunters, in this instance.

The vivacity faded from Kathleen. The bitterness and strain returned. She moved to her rifle, saw to it that a shell was in the firing chamber, and placed the weapon near at hand. She then started preparing food for their evening meal. Cold food. They built no fire that might betray their presence.

Both she and Dan watched the channel where the stream escaped from the alcove. Time passed. Sundown came. No man-hunters appeared in the opening. Dan finally rolled a cigarette, and lighted it.

Kathleen spoke. "What do you think?"

Dan shrugged. He waited until early dusk. Then, carrying Kathleen's rifle as well as the six-shooter, he waded to his waist out of the alcove and emerged cautiously into the open.

He scouted down the stream. A quarter of a mile from their hideout, he found the tracks of shod hoofs. He traced them for a distance, then made his way back to the alcove.

He saw the vast lift of spirit in Kathleen when he reappeared. "They turned back," he said. "Just as you predicted, they believed they had reached the source of the river."

He added, "You seem to be right, also, about the Shannons. If they know about this place, they haven't talked. About how far is it to their ranch?"

"Nearly two hours ride," she said. "Longer, because we'll have to be very careful. There'll still be possemen out there. They know we're somewhere near."

She was silent for a space, then added, "They might even be waiting for you at the Shannon ranch. What if it's a trap after all? By Lavinia. You may be shot down."

"That doesn't fit in with what we really believe," Dan said. "I've got to ask Lavinia Shannon why she lied when she named me as the one who killed Heber. I want you to wait here for me."

"You'd get lost and wander for hours," she said. "Regardless of that, I'm going with you." She walked close to him, looking up at him. "What good would it do to live, if I stayed here, and you never came back? I'd keep on waiting here for you—forever."

He drew her into his arms. "This isn't fair to you, Kathleen," he said huskily.

"It's the only way you can be fair, Daniel. I must go where you go, be with you always until this thing is finished. Share and share alike."

"Alex Emmons told the truth when he warned you against me," Dan said. "This sort of thing follows a man like me. Guns. Gunplay. You've had enough sadness. More than enough."

"I'll never mourn you," she said. "For, I'll always have this day, this moment, to remember. This could be my full, happy life, if it has to be that way."

She kissed him, then looked up at him, smiling. "We won't speak again of sadness or mourning. It will always be like it was today with us. We were happy here."

Dan lifted her off her feet and waltzed with her in a burst of joy. It was a moment of wildness, of soaring spirit, of vast tenderness. The somber moment faded.

This gay mood remained with them as they rode out of the alcove. Stars were pale pinpoints in a deep gray sea. As the sky darkened, they grew into glittering white diamonds. The Milky Way began to appear.

Kathleen stretched her arms toward the mystic panoply. "I'm almost reaching them," she sighed. "But they always escape me. If only I could wear them in my hair."

But, as the great black bulk of the twin buttes drew nearer, she became silent and rode very close to Dan. At times she reached out to touch him, as though to reassure herself of something very important to her.

They emerged from the gorge of the river. Dan halted his horse and pointed without speaking. A small red eye that was not a star flickered against the blackness of the range west of them. They both knew the odds were that it was the campfire of the man-hunters.

They veered far away from that danger. Presently, the breeze, which was drawing from the north, brought the scent of sheep. A dog barked, and they retreated from that peril also, for there would be a Basque sleeping in his wagon near the flock, who would be alerted by the dog.

Dan judged that the hour must be nearing midnight when Kathleen said, "There!"

The waning moon had just cleared the rims. Dan could make out the buildings of the Shannon ranch on the flat ahead. Their meandering route had brought them to the sheep ranch from the west approach.

They halted their horses and examined the night for sight or sound. Far in the range, a coyote yammered. Its comrades of the pack joined in. That strident chorus stilled.

They rode cautiously closer, pausing often to listen. The Shannon ranch was dark and silent. Dan expected to be challenged by a sheepdog, but the quiet was unbroken.

"There's nobody there," Kathleen breathed. "It's like a tomb. I'm shaking. I'm frightened."

They dismounted at a distance, tied up the horses, and began moving in warily on foot.

They halted. The pound of hoofs rose abruptly out of the silence beyond the ranch, the sound rising rapidly as a galloping horse came steadily nearer.

A six-shooter opened up, the flashes lighting the ridgepoles of the buildings. The weapon was emptied. In the vacuum that followed, Dan could hear the rattle of broken window glass following.

The thud of hoofs receded in the direction from which the rider had come. A woman was screaming something. That hysterical voice belonged to Lavinia Shannon. Her outcries broke off, and the sound of hoofs faded. The ranch was silent again, but the terror in Lavinia Shannon's voice still rang in Dan's memory.

Kathleen clung to his arm, her hands quivering. "What was that she was saying?" he asked. "It was like she was—"

"Begging!" she breathed. "Pleading! I heard the words, 'have mercy.' I couldn't make out anything more."

They moved toward the house. Faint sounds came from the interior. The chill deepened inside of Dan. What they were hearing was the grief of a woman whose despair was devastating.

The charcoal odor of the burned timbers of the two destroyed buildings was heavy in the night. Dan felt sure none of the other sheds that fringed the ranchyard held danger. Lavinia Shannon was alone with her tragedy.

He moved ahead of Kathleen and tiptoed to the main door. It opened at his touch on the latch. The house was dark, with the heartbroken sobbing of Lavinia as the only sign of life.

Dan spoke. "Lavinia Shannon!"

The sobbing broke off. He heard choked, suppressed breathing. "This is Dan Briscoe," he said. "I want to talk to you. Are you alone?"

"Briscoe?" Lavinia Shannon's instinct had been to scream the name, but her strength was not up to it, and the sound was barely audible. "Go away! Please, go away! They might still be around!"

"They?"

"I tell you to go away!"

"I doubt if whoever shot up the house is still around," Dan said. "I heard him ride in, heard him ride away. I was too far away to interfere. Were there any others? More than one?"

When she did not answer, he asked, "Are you hurt? I want to help you. I've got to talk to you."

"No, no. It would do no good. You can only help me by going away."

Kathleen spoke. "Lavinia, I'm here with Dan Briscoe. We *must* talk to you."

"You don't know what you're doing, Katey!" Lavinia Shannon sobbed. "I beg of you to go away. You'll only make matters worse."

Kathleen was weeping also. "Lavinia, you called me Katey, just like you used to when I was a child. You don't hate us any longer, do you? Both our families have been so wrong, so proud, so blind!"

She moved past Dan into the room. "Whatever it is, whatever they've done to you, we can help you," she said. "I'm coming in."

"Please, Katey!" Lavinia choked. "Don't interfere. I don't know what to do. That terrible man!"

Dan knew Kathleen had the older woman in her arms and was trying to calm her. He felt his way to a hall which led to bedrooms and the kitchen. Kathleen continued to try to soothe Lavinia Shannon, who still pleaded that she be left alone.

There was no other sound in the house. He opened doors. It was a house of big rooms, for big men. Two rooms apparently had not been used for a long time. They gave forth a dusty, airless tang. Another evidently belonged to Lavinia. The bed in the fourth room was neatly made. He was sure this was the one into which he had carried Heber Shannon the night of the shooting.

A smaller room opened off this one, and from the signs this was where little Chad Shannon had slept and played. His small bed was in disorder. But the lad was not there. Nor was there any sign of Heber Shannon.

Dan returned to the main room. Lavinia had now gained control of her emotions. Her voice still shook, however. "Again, I beg of you to go away, Mr. Briscoe!"

"Where is your son?" Dan asked. "Heber?"

"My son is dead," she said. She spoke as though she was repeating something she had rehearsed in her mind many times.

"Dead? When did he die?"

"That night he was shot. After Dr. Anderson left." She added, "We held the funeral the next afternoon."

Dan was certain she was not telling the truth. "Your grandson?" he asked abruptly. "Where is he?"

That did it. The storm Lavinia Shannon had fought back, burst into full, agonized flood. "Please! Please! Don't ask me that! They'll torture—! They'll—they'll—!"

She managed to stem the outburst. She was swaying. Kathleen steadied her. Dan lifted her in his arms. "Here!" Kathleen said, and guided him to a sofa on which he placed his burden.

He found his block of matches and located a lamp which he lighted. He waited until Lavinia was able to listen. "They've got him, haven't they?" he said gently. "The boy?"

Kathleen uttered a cry of horror. He grasped her shoulder and shook her. "Don't you go to pieces on me, too," he said. "This has got to be faced. Mrs. Shannon, you've gone through too much in your life to give in to people like that."

Lavinia seemed to find some peace of mind, now that the real cause of her travail was out in the open. Her voice steadied. "He's only a little boy," she said. "So very, very small. He must be so frightened, so terrified. I told his mother on her deathbed I'd take care of him, see that he was happy and protected. I've failed."

She looked appealingly at Dan. "They said they'd torture him if I refused to do the things they demanded."

Dan and Kathleen looked at each other, ashen-faced. Kidnaping!

"That's why you accused me of shooting your son, isn't it?" he asked gently. "They forced you to do it."

"Yes. I did what they wished. I had to have time. A chance to think. But when I heard they were going to lynch you, I just—just couldn't let them do it."

"When did they take the boy?" Dan asked.

"The next night after Heber was shot. They knew Heber was alive, and knew he had seen the man who shot him."

"Heber's alive?" Kathleen exclaimed.

"Yes. I lied when I said he had died. I even made Doc Anderson believe he had passed away and had been buried."

"Tell us what happened, step by step," Dan urged.

Lavinia fought for calmness. "Heber was able to talk that night, after you had left. He told me he had come upon this man we know as Tom Smith setting fire to the shearing shed. Another man shot Heber in the back. The two of them dragged him into the shed, leaving him to be burned alive, but he managed to crawl out to where you found him."

"Where's Heber now?" Kathleen asked.

"I had the Basques move him out of the house. They're taking care of him in a sheep wagon, hidden out in the range. You see, Heber saw the second man too. The one who shot him. It came to me that they would come back to silence him when they found out he was still alive. He's hurt bad, but I'm hoping he'll be all right in time."

"Who shot him?" Dan asked. "Or, maybe I already know."

"Maybe you do," Lavinia said. "It was Obie Willit."

Again Dan and Kathleen looked at each other. "Of course," Kathleen said bitterly. "We've been such fools, Lavinia."

"You mean you know about Obie too, Katey?"

"Yes, but only lately. Too late, I'm afraid. We all

139

thought Obie was our friend. Instead he was out to ruin us by setting us at each other's throats."

"I knew for some time that Obie had changed," Lavinia said. "But I never realized how much he had changed until that night. Then the whole thing was clear."

"That explains the three sulled horses," Dan said.

He told them of scouting Obie Willit's house in Flat Butte late that night after Heber Shannon had been shot, and of finding three horses that had been hard-ridden.

"Obie, Shep Sand and Gid Marko all were likely in on stampeding the beef holdout at Spanish Bell right after dark that night," he said. "Then Marko must have been the one who split off, went to Royal House and killed Kathleen's father. Obie and Sand headed for the Shannon ranch where they fired the shearing shed and shot Heber."

"But why——?" Kathleen began.

". . . Why did Obie suddenly come out in the open, instead of hiding back his hired gunmen? My guess is that Sand and Marko forced Obie to tar himself with the same brush—murder. Obie also probably realized he had to get the thing finished. He must have known he couldn't get away with his scheme much longer. He figured that night's work would be the finishing blow for both Spanish Bell and the Shannon ranch."

"What impelled you to scout Obie's house that night?"

"A hunch mostly. I guessed that they'd show up there. Maybe to set up an alibi, but, more likely, it was a matter of money. Knowing the kind of men Sand and Marko are, I figured they'd want to be paid in cash right away for that kind of a night's work. I believe they demanded a lot more than Obie had promised them. I suspect they wanted to be cut in as partners on the whole affair. At least on the profits. It sounded to me like they were quarreling. Sand and Marko evidently didn't make an issue of it, for they rode back to Shacktown."

He turned to Lavinia. "You say they took the boy the next night?"

"I was alone with Chad," she said dully. "I never dreamed they'd be vicious enough to steal a little boy. They burst in right after I had put Chad to bed. They were masked, but I knew them. They were the ones you call Shep Sand and Gid Marko. They had really come to kill

Heber. When they didn't find him in the house they knew I wasn't telling the truth when I said he had died. They started to try to force me to tell where he was. They burned me with a hot poker."

She spread open the palms of her hands. She had contrived bandages over blisters. Kathleen uttered a moan of anger and sympathy.

"When they realized I'd never talk," Lavinia went on quietly, "they found a better way of torturing me. They took Chad away with them. They said that if I ever wanted to see him alive again, I must follow orders."

"Orders?"

"Obie Willit, himself, came here the next day. Butter wouldn't melt in his mouth, but he knew I was on to him. He acted as though nothing had happened. He told me there was no doubt but that you were the man who had shot Heber. He said everyone knew the Royals had hired you to wipe out the Shannons, and that those two gunmen in Shacktown were also being paid by the Royals. He told me the sheriff was arriving by stage, and that I must go to town with him and swear out a warrant that you had shot Heber."

She began to sob again. "Then he asked about Chad's health. The filthy devil! He said he hoped the boy was all right. I understood. I had my orders. I knew I'd never see Chad alive again unless I obeyed."

She looked at Dan. "They knew they had to get rid of you, Mr. Briscoe. They were afraid of you. They organized that lynch mob at Shacktown to get you out of the way forever."

"Have you any idea at all as to where they might be hiding your grandson?" Dan asked.

"No. I don't even know if—if he's—he's alive."

Lavinia could not go on. Kathleen led her to her bedroom. Dan, the chill still in his blood, stood, trying to think. He was in for an even deeper chill. The living room in which he stood had borne the brunt of the bullet attack. Two windows had been smashed, the glass scattered over the carpet.

He noticed a blue object lying beneath a rocking chair. He picked it up. It was a blue bandanna neckerchief that had been knotted around a stone in order to give it weight so that it could be hurled through the window.

Inside the sling was a ragged scrap of paper which bore a penciled message. The note, written with exaggerated crudeness, said:

> if you shannons dew any talkin us will
> send you the kids whole skelp nekst time

The paper bore a dark blotch. Stiffened blood. Matted to it was a tuft of fine, tawny hair. It had been torn with brutal strength from a scalp. A child's scalp.

He fought nausea. The bandanna was of the common type that came in a variety of colors, and which nearly all riders carried as neckerchiefs for use against dust or heat. This one, apparently, had never been worn. It bore the creases of storage. It retained the smell of newness.

He inspected the paper. It was of heavy, smooth brown stock. He decided it was the kind in which meat was wrapped at a store counter.

He heard Kathleen returning, and thrust the items in his pocket.

"I tried to prevail on Lavinia to get some sleep," she said as she entered. "I hope she can make it. She—" She paused, looking closely at him. "What is it?" she asked.

"What do you mean?"

"I don't exactly know," she said. "There's something in your eyes. Something terrible."

"Why shouldn't there be?" he said. "I better fetch in the horses. If you could rustle up a bite of food, it might help all of us. And, above all, coffee."

He hurried out before she could question him. He brought in the two mounts and fed and led them to water. When he returned to the house, coffee was boiling in the kitchen and bacon was sputtering in a skillet. Kathleen was working at the huge cooking stove. Lavinia sat at the kitchen table, pale and hollow-eyed. Sleep had evaded her, but, for once, she was letting younger hands take charge.

"I'll have it on the table in a few minutes," Kathleen told him. "You can wash up at the bench outside."

Again she searched his face with her eyes. What she saw did nothing to allay the terror that was growing in her. She asked a silent, demanding question with her lips. But he only shook his head in refusal, and escaped to the wash bench.

When he returned, he spoke to Lavinia. "Make sure Heber is guarded every minute. Send word to the Basques to never leave him alone, and for them to keep their guns handy and be ready to shoot. Obie's men will still be hunting him. They probably don't believe he's dead. He's the only witness who can destroy them, as long as he's alive."

He moved to Kathleen, took her in his arms, and kissed her. "You're beautiful," he said. "It would be wonderful to go through life with you. No man could ask for anything more. I just want you to know how I feel about you."

She suddenly tried to cling to him, realizing that what he was saying was that this might be a final parting.

"No, my darling!" she said, the tears beginning. "Oh, no. Why? Oh, why? Does it have to be?"

"I know of no other way," Dan said. "And there's no time to lose."

He spoke to Lavinia. "Your grandson is still alive, but that is all I know. I'll try to bring him back to you."

He kissed Kathleen again. "Wait for me. I *want* to come back."

She released him. She stood, the tears shining on her cheeks, watching him ride away. When he last looked back, she was still standing in the ranchyard, her hands pressed to her breast to ease the grief that tore at her.

CHAPTER FIFTEEN

The sun was coming up when Dan returned across the fence line into Spanish Bell range. Only one breakfast fire lifted smoke from the hovels of Shacktown as he passed by on the opposite side of the river. The inhabitants had no ambition for early rising.

He studied the place, concentrating on the gabled house and the adjoining store building. He saw no sign of activity there.

He headed toward Royal House, avoiding the road where he might encounter someone who would recognize him and put a posse on his trail.

He still carried the six-shooter he had taken from Jed Jenkins. It was a nickel-plated .44 with a wooden handle that had been scarred and chipped by much use. It probably had seen service at pounding coffee beans and driving tent stakes in overnight camps. It lacked balance, and Dan doubted if its action could be trusted. Jed Jenkins' principal task as a deputy probably had been that of serving court summonses and tax notices.

The sun was an hour high when he crossed the irrigation bridge and dismounted at the gallery of Royal House. The fragrance of breakfast came from the house. Alex Emmons appeared, followed by Emilio and Josefa.

Alex peered at Dan's bristle of whiskers and red-rimmed eyes. It came to Dan that he must have the look of a fugitive. The wolf look. Alex framed a question, but Dan answered it before it was uttered.

"Kathleen's all right. A lot of other things are not. Too many to talk over right now. I came here to get something that belongs to me."

He spoke to Emilio. "I'd thank you if you'd catch up a fresh horse for me. This one has seen a lot of miles."

He walked into the house and to the main room where Bill Royal had been shot. Alex and Josefa followed and stood silent. He pulled open the drawer in the highboy that Bill Royal had been trying to reach when the bullet had ended his life. He drew out the belt and the two silver-mounted .44s and strapped them on. He left Jed Jenkins' pistol lying on the table.

Josefa made the sign of the cross. "I will pray for you, señor," she said, and began to weep. *"Vaya con Dios!* Go with God!"

"Thank you, señora," Dan said. "It's a little boy. Chad Shannon. They've got him and are torturing him. His grandmother will suffer even more unless something is done right away to get him away from them. They will kill him unless I can find him in a hurry."

Josefa embraced him. "I will light a candle for you. I know you go into great danger."

Dan walked to the kitchen, poured a mug of strong coffee from the pot on the stove, and drank it while Emilio was bringing in a fresh horse for him.

He walked to the gallery, shook hands with Emilio, and mounted. Baldy Strapp, still recuperating from the beating the gunmen had given him, hobbled to the door, supporting himself on a cane, and stood watching.

144

Alex appeared. He had put on his holstered, black-handled pistol and had a rifle slung in an arm. He swung onto the horse which Emilio had used in rounding up a mount for Dan.

He looked at Dan and said, "Let's go."

"Stay out of this," Dan said.

"I've grown a lot older just lately," Alex said. "I'm going with you this time—all the way. You can't stop me. Don't try. I don't know what this is all about, but you can bring me up to date while we're riding."

Dan studied him and nodded. He swung his horse around and headed out of the ranchyard. Alex rode at his side.

"Where do we go first?" Alex asked.

"To Obie Willit's store," Dan said.

Alex twisted in the saddle, staring. "Obie Willit's?"

Dan tersely repeated the story. He drew from his pocket the message written on the scrap of paper. He watched the revulsion that came into Alex's face. And the fury.

"I've got a few questions to ask Obie," he said.

"My God!" Alex breathed. "Not Obie Willit? But—"

Dan nodded. "It's easy to see now, all of a sudden."

"Not exactly all of a sudden," Alex said bitterly. "It seemed to have been in the back of my mind for some time. That speech he made to that bunch of lynchers the other night clinched it for me. It didn't ring true."

He added, "But kidnaping a child. How could a man like Obie Willit ever fall that low?"

"Step by step," Dan said. "First it was ambition to amount to something, I imagine. That meant getting his hands on money. Avarice. Then hiring gunmen to terrorize the Royals and the Shannons. Then murder. Now this."

Alex's lips were hard-set, ashen. "If you don't get the right answers to the questions you aim to ask Obie . . . ?"

Dan did not reply, but kept riding steadily ahead. Alex grasped his arm. "Obie's mine," he said hoarsely. "I'm the one to make him talk. That would only be right. Don't you realize what we've been through—what he's done to us?"

"You'd kill him," Dan said. "He's got to talk first. I'm the one to handle this."

Avoiding the trails, they approached Flat Butte from the east. From a timbered rise they studied the town. The hour was approaching noon. The sun blazed down on Flat

Butte's dusty street. Only a few citizens moved on the sidewalks. The tie rails were occupied by three saddle horses, and a rickety top buggy.

"From the looks," Dan said, "the sheriff and his hunters are still out in the range. We'll go in on foot. We'll stroll past that dobe shack where the goats are grazing, and to the mercantile from the side street. We'll be less likely to attract attention, coming in from that direction."

"What if Obie ain't in his store?" Alex asked.

"He'll be there."

"How come you're so all-fired sure?"

"From what I've seen of him, he's a man of habit. Today, above all days, he'll be very sure to follow his regular schedule, so that nothing will seem out of the ordinary."

They tied up their horses. Moving casually, they reached the deserted lane that flanked the mercantile without being challenged. Dan peered into the street. They waited a minute or two until the coast was clear, then walked without haste into the open street, mounted the plank steps and moved through the door into the store.

Obie Willit was alone in his mercantile at this hour of slack trading. He was operating the crank of a slicing machine which stood on a counter, and to which he had clamped a length of sandwich meat. The whirling blade, moving back and forth, was lopping off neat circles of the meat. He had placed a handful of crackers and a wedge of cheese nearby. Apparently, he was about to partake of a noontime snack.

He halted the revolving blade, and squinted against the glare of sunlight from the street in an attempt to identify the two figures that had entered.

"Howdy, men!" he boomed in his hearty voice. "A mighty warm day, ain't it? I was just fixin' to——"

Then he recognized them, and instantly knew their purpose. Slices of meat and crackers scattered as he tried to seize something beneath the counter.

He did not make it. Dan dove over the counter, clamped his arms around his quarry, and drove him staggering against the shelves.

Willit was tremendously powerful. He strained, and might have broken Dan's grip. Alex came up, tapped Willit sharply on the head with the muzzle of his pistol, then

146

jammed the bore of the weapon savagely into the big man's stomach.

"Stand quiet, or I'll blast your guts through your backbone," Alex gritted.

Dan stepped back. A shotgun lay beneath the counter. This was what Willit had been attempting to get his hands on. Farther along hung a six-shooter in a holster.

"All right, Obie," Dan said. "Better do exactly what Alex tells you. My only worry is that he might kill you before I can ask you a few questions."

Willit tried to bluster it out. "Do you know what you're doin', Alex? This here man is wanted fer murder. Are you aimin' on goin' outlaw with him?"

"We came here to do a little shopping," Dan said.

"Shoppin'?" Willit was trying to be dominating, but there was in his eyes a ghastly fear. Dan knew the store owner, in his mind, was raking over details, trying to place his finger on whatever mistake he might have made.

"We're in the market for a little boy," Dan said. "Chad Shannon."

"I don't know what you're talkin' about!" Willit said.

Dan slapped him. Slapped him hard. The blow staggered the big man once more.

"Buffalo him if he tries to get away, Alex," Dan said. "But don't kill him—not yet, at least."

He walked down the store to the meat cooler where beef quarters and smoked products were on display back of glass windows. A roll of wrapping paper stood on the counter near a chopping block, mounted on its steel cutter.

Dan drew from his pocket the scrap of paper on which had been written the message to Lavinia Shannon. He compared color and texture. They were identical.

He crossed the room to the drygoods section. Searching among the shelves, he located a stack of bandanna neckerchiefs. Some had red backgrounds, some green, others blue. The blue neckerchiefs were duplicates of the one he drew from his pocket, even to the factory creases.

He turned. Willit had been watching. The big man's face was no longer ruddy. It held a gray, lifeless hue.

"Where is he?" Dan asked.

"What air you talkin' about?" Willit demanded hoarsely.

Dan walked across the room. Once more he swung the palm of his right hand. The blow knocked Willit off his feet. He crashed to the floor back of the counter, and lay there, looking up with eyes that were very terrified and very pig-like.

"Where is he?" Dan repeated.

Willit did not answer. He merely stared, a mound of flesh, looking up in terror at Dan.

With both hands, Dan grasped the man by the shaggy hair and lifted his weight bodily to his feet. Willit uttered a moan of pain. He tried to lower his head and butt Dan in the stomach, swinging pudgy fists at the same time. Dan blocked the blows and drove a knee into Willit's face.

"What have you done with Chad Shannon?" he asked again.

His knee had broken Willit's nose and mashed his lips against his teeth. Blood was flowing.

He heard a sound and glanced over his shoulder. Kathleen stood in the door from the street. She was ashen, appalled.

Alex was pale also. He had unconsciously lowered his six-shooter, and stood as though he could not believe what he was seeing.

Kathleen spoke, her voice very faint. "Don't!"

"How did you get here?" he demanded.

"I knew you were coming here," she said.

"Leave," Dan said. "This is no place for you."

"Is this—this necessary?"

"Yes. There's no time to lose."

He gave her the paper on which the kidnapers had fixed the tuft of child's scalp. She swayed a little as she realized the significance of what she was seeing. She fought back faintness.

"Where is the boy, Obie?" he again asked, and still did not raise his voice. "You wrote that note there at the meat counter, and gave Sand or Marko that neckerchief from your stock over there. Are you the one who tore that ugly piece of scalp from a child's head?"

"I swear I don't know nothin' about——!"

"Is he dead? Have you murdered him?"

"I tell you I don't know——"

"Quit lying!" Dan said. He spoke over his shoulder to Kathleen. "You must leave. This isn't going to be pretty."

148

"If you can stand it, I can," she said pallidly. She closed the door in the face of a woman with a market basket on her arm, and bolted it. She drew the window blinds.

"Obie," she said. "You're going to tell us where you've taken Chad Shannon."

"That's right, Obie," Dan said. "I've never done to anyone what I'm ready to do to you. This is the first time I've ever dealt with a thing who would injure a child for the sake of money. Torture is out of my line, but in your case, I've only started. I don't consider you human, or even animal."

He shoved Willit to the counter where the meat slicer stood. He freed the section of meat from the clamps that had held it in place, then dragged Willit's hand onto the rack.

"Clamp him down," he ordered Alex. "Tight."

Alex, still ashen, complied, twisting the thumb screws, and the bar closed down on Willit's hand, holding his fingers in the path of the cutting blade.

"You can't!" Willit croaked.

"Try me and see," Dan said. "I'll take one finger at a time. Talk! Where is he? Where's little Chad Shannon?"

Willit began to moan and plead. Dan turned the crank, and the thin blade began to revolve and move toward Willit's fingers. It drew a thin line of crimson. Dan reversed the crank, and the blade retreated.

"Last chance for that finger, Obie," he said.

Obie Willit broke. "Don't!" he begged. "You devil! I only want to say one thing. Takin' the boy wasn't my idea. Why, I wouldn't harm a man or woman in the world, let alone a—"

"You pig!" Dan said. "It was *all* your idea."

"It was them that done it!" Willit wailed.

"Them? Shep Sand and Gid Marko?"

"Now, I wouldn't know who you mean by—"

"You knew who they were when you brought them into this country," Dan said. "This is your last chance. Where is that boy?"

Again the blade advanced. An inch or two more and Willit would lose a finger.

"Wait!" Willit choked. "Wait! They got him in the store in Shacktown. In the root dugout."

Dan halted the blade. He gazed at the cringing man.

149

"That better be the truth, Obie," he said. "If not, I'll come back."

He made sure the clamps that held Willit's hand were tight. A roll of heavy twine stood nearby. Kathleen helped bind Willit's free arm to his side. Then they lashed him to the counter, his arm still held in the slicing machine.

"Keep remembering that kidnaping is a hanging offense," Dan said.

He heard the thud of hoofs receding in the street. The front door had been unbolted and stood open. Alex Emmons was missing.

Kathleen ran to the door. "He's taken my horse!" she exclaimed. "Now, where is he going?"

Dan burst past her. "To Shacktown! Where else? To shoot it out with Sand and Marko!"

He ran into the street, heading toward the livery. Kathleen tried to keep pace with him, but failed. Doors opened, heads appeared along the street.

Someone yelled, "It's thet gunman from Spanish Bell! Diamond Dan Briscoe what shot Heber Shannon!"

"Stay out of this!" Dan shouted. "Heber Shannon is alive! Go to the mercantile and take a look at Obie Willit! But, don't turn him loose. He's going to hang for what he's done. Ask him about little Chad Shannon."

That halted any who might have thought of trying to stop him. The presence of Kathleen, who was running in desperate pursuit of Dan, also gave them a pause.

Dan raced into the tunnel of the livery barn. The hostler ducked out of sight into a stall. Four horses were in the stalls. Saddles and bridles hung on racks. Dan seized rigging, and picked out the biggest and most powerfully built horse of the four and began saddling. Kathleen arrived gasping as he swung into the saddle.

"Thet hawss belongs to Obie Willit," the hostler yelled from his hiding place. "This here livery is owned by Obie an' he sure is hard on hawss thieves. You'll git your neck stretched if'n he ketches up with you."

"You'll find two saddled Spanish Bell horses out in the shinnery east of town," Dan said. "Bring them in and feed and care for them."

Kathleen tried to stop him as he rode out of the livery, but he only shook his head and pushed the horse to a gallop.

The hoofmarks of the animal Alex was riding were deep in the road. However, he had such a start, Dan doubted there was any chance of overtaking him. Dan also discovered he had made a mistake in judging the capabilities of the horse he had picked out in haste. It was big and powerful, but was proving to be heavy-footed and slow.

Reaching the fork near the river, he glimpsed Alex heading toward Shacktown. He was nearly a mile away. Then timber cut off the view.

Looking back, Dan saw Kathleen come into view at least half a mile behind him.

Dan put his animal to its best speed. Timber continued to mask the view. When he emerged into the open, half a mile from the scatter of habitations, he saw Alex's riderless horse, reins down, standing in the hot sun in the empty road near the gabled house in the heart of Shacktown.

Alex was not in sight.

CHAPTER SIXTEEN

Shacktown seemed deserted as its makeshift walls and crooked chimneys drew close at hand. The only sign of life was Alex's drooping, lathered horse. If any of the inhabitants were at home, they stayed hidden. Not a face showed.

Dan dismounted and stood for a moment beside his mount, listening. The afternoon breeze brought the sound of bootheels crunching in hot soil. He was unable to locate the direction.

The flat-roofed structure, which bore the label of a store, was hidden from his view by a shack to his left. Obie Willit had said that Chad Shannon was being held captive there.

He heard Kathleen's horse arrive. He glanced over his shoulder and waved a command for her to stay at a distance. She obeyed, halting her horse and dismounting. He saw vast fear for him in her attitude, but she did not speak or make any attempt to dissuade him.

The silence was ended by a gunshot, so near at hand it was savage on his nerves. He began running. His brace of guns were drawn, the hammers cocked.

A second, heavy report came. He rounded the corner of the hovel and halted, crouching, his pistols weaving back and forth. But no target was in sight.

Alex Emmons was sprawled face-down not far from the door of the store. His six-shooter lay on the hot earth beside him, his hand near it as though he had been trying to fire it when he had fallen. The stain of blood darkened the earth beneath him.

The tang of burned gunpowder was still strong in the air, but there was no way of knowing from where the shots had been fired.

Kathleen came running into view. She screamed wildly, grievously, when she saw Alex's body.

"Stay back!" Dan commanded. She obeyed, halting, then backing slowly to safer distance.

Dan crossed the open space between the two buildings, his eyes continuing to search for a target. He stepped over Alex's body and got his back to the wall of the store, a pace from its door.

He doubted if the shots had come from this structure. He kept his eyes on the larger house and its windows where the green blinds flapped slowly in the push of the hot wind.

The gabled house had been built as cheaply as possible. He doubted if there was plaster inside. Nothing but unfinished walls and ceilings and plank floors. The lower sash in the lone window above the lean-to kitchen was raised. The door of the kitchen stood partly open. There were no windows in the rear wall of the kitchen. If killers were in the house, they must fire from the door or from the window above.

He believed Alex had been shot down from the upper window, rather than from the kitchen door. Perhaps from both vantage points. Alex had walked into a trap!

A shadow moved at the window He fired instantly with one gun. The bullet struck the sash, and must have showered whoever was inside with splinters.

A six-shooter flamed in the window, the report almost overlapping the explosion of his own weapon. But the slug went wide, the gunman's aim upset by his shot.

He dove for the nearby doorway of the store. Bullets bracketed him. Guns were roaring in the window of the gabled house and in the kitchen door.

The door of the store was driven wide open by the slugs that smashed into its panels. He plunged flat on his face into the building and rolled aside, out of sight.

He waited for the pain and shock to come. He could not believe it when he realized he had come unscathed through that sleet of metal.

The dingy interior of the structure was lighted only by small, grimy windows, set in three walls. The doorway was the only opening in the front wall. Barrels and packing cases were spread in disorder. A plank counter, set on boxes, flanked the wall to the right. A few shelves held a scant collection of canned staples. Sacks containing sprouting potatoes, onions, and turnips leaned drunkenly against a wall.

"Chad!" he called. "Chad Shannon!"

He waited, listening. He believed he heard faint, thumping sounds, but it might have been only the thud of his pulse. He moved on hands and knees along the plank floor.

The sound was real! It came from below! He expected the gunmen to appear at the door, but they did not come. Obie Willit had said the child was being held in a root dugout. He searched around at the rear in the semi-gloom, and found the entrance. It was covered by a few planks and a blanket.

Clearing the opening, he peered into a musty excavation. He could hear faint, gurgling sounds. He lowered himself into the opening, and found it less than his height. There he also found Chad Shannon.

The lad was gagged, his small wrists lashed behind him, and his ankles tied with leather thongs. Dan lifted him into the shabby light of the room.

"You're all right now," he whispered.

Dan worked the gag free, and, after some difficulty, managed to loosen the bonds that had been tied brutally tight.

Chad Shannon tried to talk, but failed. His small face was puffed and discolored. He was caked with dust and his hair was matted with dried blood. He had been beaten. His legs bore welts made by a quirt.

Dan began chafing circulation in the lad's arms and legs, hoping that his efforts were in time.

He shouted, "Kathleen! Circle around to the back of the

store! Stay down so they can't shoot at you from the house. I've got the boy!"

He smashed the glass from the window at the rear. Kathleen soon appeared at the opening. "Here he is," Dan said, lifting the boy into her arms through the window. "What's left of him."

She cuddled Chad Shannon in her arms. "You're safe now, darling," she choked.

Chad Shannon managed to talk. He had recovered both his voice and his spunk. "Them damned bad men!" he mumbled. "I'll pay 'em off when I grow up."

Dan looked at the lad's bruises and emaciation. "Sand and Marko are forted up in the house," he said. "Don't let them get a shot at you. Take the boy to his grandmother."

He started to turn away from the window. "No!" Kathleen protested desperately. "The law will take care of this!"

"Like it took care of what's gone on in the past?" Dan said harshly. "Look at that boy! Look at what they did to him! We can't take a chance on those two ever getting turned loose in the world again."

"Isn't Alex's death enough?" she sobbed. "Think of me! I can't lose you, too."

"You know I'm right," Dan said. "You know this has to be tried, that I just can't walk away from it. And you know how much I love you."

He left the window and moved to the door of the store, peering warily through the slit between the door and its frame. Alex's body lay motionless. The window and the door of the house seemed vacant.

"I'm coming after you, Sand!" he called. "And you, Marko. This is Dan Briscoe."

Such was the fury in him. Such was the urge to pay them for what they had done to Chad Shannon. And to Lavinia Shannon and to Kathleen and all the others who had died or had been baited into hating their friends.

There was no answer. Dan leaped through the door, and ran, twisting and ducking, toward the house firing one gun as he moved. The upper window and the lower door belched gunflame. Bullets grazed him, plucked at his sleeves, plowed spurts of dust around his boots. They had not expected his maneuver and had been startled into shooting frenziedly.

He survived and reached the rear wall of the kitchen an

154

arm's length from the open door. He flattened there, hidden from the man in the upper room by the eaves of the lean-to.

He reloaded his six-shooter from the shells in the loops of the gunbelt. Silence came. Then he could hear them moving stealthily in the creaky house, moving to better positions, no doubt.

Dry tumbleweeds grew against the walls of the structure, or had lodged there. He found his matches and touched them off. They burst into swift, crackling flame.

He raced along the side of the house to the front corner. The weeds might or might not ignite the house in their brief moment of lurid life.

But he was too late. Sand and Marko were taking no chances of being trapped in a burning house. They had made their move ahead of him and had stampeded out of the house and through the door into the open.

Sand evidently had been the one in the kitchen, for he led the way. He was running toward a neighboring shack which was crookedly constructed of pine poles and mud-chinked slabs of broken rock. The occupants of this hovel had already fled to a safer distance, terrified by the shooting.

Sand ducked around the corner of the shack, but Marko, who had been forced to race from the second floor, was a dozen strides short of cover.

"Marko!" Dan shouted, stepping into the open.

Gideon Marko turned, crouching and ducking aside, firing all in one motion.

Dan fired at the same instant. A drift of dust came from the back of Marko's coat as the slug tore entirely through his chest and emerged. The man's lean body hit the ground, and twisted there in a rigadoon of death. The shot he had aimed at Dan had missed.

Dan raced toward the hovel where Sand had taken shelter. He realized that his opponent was crouched at the corner, waiting for him to appear. Sand would have a split second advantage before Dan could locate him, and that might be edge enough.

Dan swerved, circling the structure to the rear. He heard crunching footsteps and knew Sand was shifting to meet this new point of attack.

He halted. He tried to suppress his breathing. He succeeded only for a few seconds, for his lungs, driven to their utmost by the strain of this moment, demanded their toll. But, during that interval, he could hear Sand's lungs laboring.

Kathleen called something, entreatingly. He could not make out the words, but knew she was pleading with him to break off this duel that was sure to end in the death of one or the other. Or both. He did not answer.

Shep Sand lifted his voice. "I'm willin' to call it quits if you are, Briscoe."

"Are you the one who used the quirt on the boy?" Dan responded.

"There's no sense in us shootin' this out," Sand answered. "We're two of a kind. Doin' only what we was paid for. If it hadn't been me, it'd have been somebody else. Maybe you."

"This is the last time—for you," Dan said.

He tossed a pebble, lifting a spurt of dust at the corner of the hovel. It was an old trick to concentrate an opponent's attention on one spot while the attack came from another point.

Shep Sand knew all the tricks. Dan gambled that the man would expect him to recircle the shack in an attempt to strike from the original point.

He arose and rushed, crouching, to the corner where he had thrown the pebble. He began shooting with both guns the instant he rounded the corner.

He was staking his life on the gamble. And he had guessed wrong. Sand had the advantage. He was not waiting alongside the hovel. He had found cover back of a sizable driftwood tree that had been dragged from the river to serve as a handy source of firewood.

Sand was shooting also, flattened back of his breastwork a dozen yards from the hovel. He had a brace of pistols and both weapons were blazing. He was a man who had lived in cold blood, without compassion and conscience. He had lived by the gun. He had accepted the fact, no doubt, that some day he might die by the gun. There was in him a bravado, an indifference that was fatalistic.

Dan kept racing into the maw of Sand's flaming guns. His own pistols were roaring. There was now no turning back for either of them.

The distance was only a dozen strides. An infinity. Dan

knew he was hit, but kept going. And kept shooting. He had only Sand's pasty, black-mustached face as his target.

He saw a bullet hole appear in Sand's forehead. He saw life dissolve from the man, even though Sand managed to rock back the hammer of his right gun and fire a final shot whose powder flame scorched Dan's cheek.

Dan's momentum carried him sprawling across the log and over his foe's body. He fell heavily and lay there. He knew he had been hit by more than one bullet and he only wanted to lie there and rest. He had carried the weight of the world for a time—the kind of a world he wanted to live in. All he wanted now was to surrender the burden.

Kathleen came running. Amazingly, Dan saw that Alex Emmons was at her side. Alex was blood-stained, but he seemed very much alive.

Kathleen was kneeling at his side, babbling wild words. She kissed him, her lips cold as ice.

"Let's try that again," Dan heard himself mumbling. "That's good medicine."

Then the pain began. After that he had unrelated, distorted impressions. Of long periods of blackness. Of hearing the dry voice of Dr. Anderson saying testily: "Four slugs in him, and all he'll get out of it are scars to show to his grandchildren." Of hearing Kathleen's voice, speaking soothingly, warmly to him. Of knowing her hand lay in his. Of hearing Alex say, "He was born under a lucky star."

It was nearing sundown two days later when he came out of it for keeps. He lay in a room at Spanish Bell. Kathleen was looking down at him. She was wearing a pale yellow dress that did something for her hair and eyes.

"Don't just stand there," he said, finding his voice a croak. "Tell me what happened."

She kissed him. She was a little hysterical. "It's all over," she sobbed. "And you're alive. You're going to stay alive."

"Of course," he said. "Sand? Marko?"

She didn't answer. None was needed. "How about Obie Willit?" he asked.

"In jail in Flag by this time," she said. "The sheriff left with him by stage yesterday. He'll be tried for both murder and kidnaping."

She went to the door and called. "He's awake!"

Alex appeared. He wore an arm in a sling and moved

cautiously. He grinned. "I sorta stopped a piece of lead with my left shoulder blade," he said. "It knocked all the sass out of me for a few minutes. But the doc says I'll soon be able to hold a poker hand and hug the girls ag'in."

Lavinia Shannon came into the room, and she looked years younger. With her was her grandson.

Chad Shannon was bathed and scrubbed, and wearing his bench-made boots, range hat, and tailored garb. He walked to the side of the bed, and extended a hand. "Shake, cowboy," he said. "Gran'maw told me to be sure an' thank you an' Alex fer what you did." He looked around, and seemed disappointed.

"What's wrong, pardner?" Dan asked.

"I wanted to see them guns o' yours," Chad said. "I hear they're really somethin'. Silver-trimmed an' purty as a paint pony. An' cost a lot o' money."

Kathleen spoke. "Nobody," she stated, "will ever see those guns again."

"Aw, shucks!" the boy lamented. "I was hopin' I could buy 'em from Dan after I growed up, an' had made a lot o' money."

"Never!" Kathleen said. "Never!"

She added, "Not until Judgment Day will anybody see those guns."

"Not until another Judgment Day, at least," Alex Emmons spoke. "And, most likely, it'll never come."

Cliff Farrell was born in Zanesville, Ohio, where earlier Zane Grey had been born. Following graduation from high school, Farrell became a newspaper reporter. Over the next decade he worked his way west by means of a string of newspaper jobs and for thirty-one years was employed, mostly as sports editor, for the *Los Angeles Examiner*. He would later claim that he began writing for pulp magazines because he grew bored with journalism. His first Western stories were written for *Cowboy Stories* in 1926 and his byline was A. Clifford Farrell. By 1928 this byline was abbreviated to Cliff Farrell, and this it remained for the rest of his career. In 1933 Farrell was invited to contribute a story for the first issue of *Dime Western*. He soon became a regular contributor to this magazine and to *Star Western* as well. In fact, many months he would have a short novel in both magazines. Farrell became such a staple at Popular Publications that by the end of the 1930s he was contributing as much as 400,000 words a year to their various Western magazines. In all, Farrell wrote nearly 600 stories for the magazine market. His earliest Western fiction tended to stress action and gun play, but increasingly his stories began to focus on characters in historical situations and the problems faced by those characters. *Follow the New Grass* (1954) was Farrell's first Western novel, a story concerned with a desperate battle over grazing rights in the Cheyenne Indian reserve. It was followed by *West with the Missouri* (1955), an exciting story of riverboats, gamblers, and gunmen. *Fort Deception* (1960), *Ride the Wild Country* (1963), *The Renegade* (1970), and *The Devil's Playground* (1976) are among the best of Farrell's later Western novels. *Desperate Journey*, a first collection of Cliff Farrell's Western short stories, has also been published.

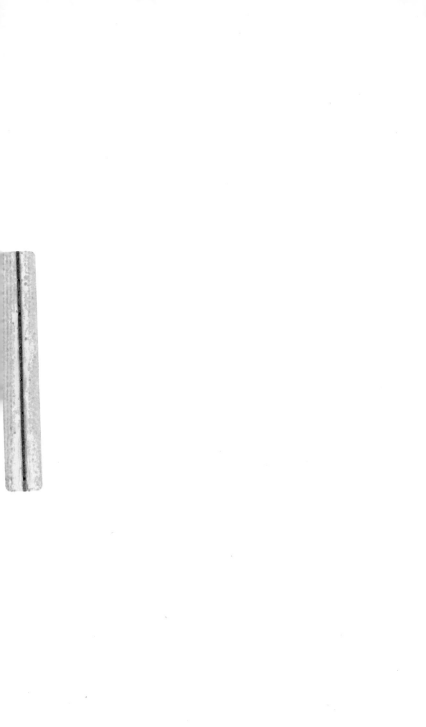